Prai

M000282971

"Wood and Baxter have delivered a stunning tale that reminds of an early Stephen King's talent for the macabre with a pinch of Graham Masterton's flair for witchcraft and terror. A sinister tale of black magic and horror – not for the faint hearted."

Greig Beck, bestselling author of *Beneath the Dark Ice* and *Black Mountain*

"When Grant Shipman returns to Wallens' Gap for his father's funeral, he discovers a curious book and a supernatural relic hidden from the malevolent townsfolk, who shelter generations of malignant secrets. After his friend Cassie is kidnapped and his own life increasingly threatened, Grant must confront the powers of darkness, a demon summoned for the ultimate sacrifice.

With mysterious rituals, macabre rites and superb supernatural action scenes, Wood and Baxter deliver a fast-paced horror thriller."

J.F.Penn, author of the bestselling *ARKANE* thriller series

"Wood and Baxter have taken on the classic black magic/cult conspiracy subgenre, chucked in a toxic mix of weirdness, creepshow chills and action, and created a tale that reads like a
latter-day Hammer Horror thriller. Nice, dark fun."

Robert Hood, author of *Immaterial* and *Fragments of a Broken Land: Valarl Undead*

Works by Alan Baxter

The Isiah Duology
RealmShift
MageSign

Stand-Alone Works
Ghost of the Black: A 'Verse Full of Scum
Dark Rite (with David Wood)

Works by David Wood

The Dane Maddock Adventures
Dourado
Cibola
Quest
Icefall
Buccaneer
Atlantis (forthcoming)
Freedom (Origins Series)

Stand-Alone Works
Into the Woods (with David S. Wood)
Callsign: Queen (with Jeremy Robinson)
Dark Rite (with Alan Baxter)

Apocalypse Tales
The Zombie-Driven Life
The 7 Habits of Highly Infective Zombies (forthcoming)

The Dunn Kelly Mysteries
You Suck
Bite Me (Forthcoming)

Writing as David Debord
The Silver Serpent
Keeper of the Mists
The Gates of Iron (forthcoming)

DARK RITE

Alan Baxter

David Wood

Dark Rite by David Wood and Alan Baxter

Copyright 2013 by David Wood and Alan Baxter

ISBN: 978-1-940095-00-4

Published April, 2013 by Gryphonwood Press
www.gryphonwoodpress.com

Dedication

Dedicated to our loyal
ThrillerCast listeners.

Chapter 1

The unrelenting blanket of green shrouded the world as far as the eye could see. Only a sprinkling of snow atop the highest peaks broke the monotony. Somewhere in this wilderness was the turnoff to Wallen's Gap. At least, that's what the map promised, though the GPS had other ideas. If the device was to be believed, the little town sat isolated between two mountains to the west with no means of ingress or egress. It was as if the forest had wrapped its arms around the town and refused to let it go.

His cell phone vibrated and he took it out, surprised he actually had coverage in the middle of nowhere. Voicemail. He must have caught a brief moment of reception. He punched up the message and pressed the phone to his ear.

Grant, it's Suzanne. I was hoping you'd answer. Listen, I know this is a bad time and all, but I couldn't bring myself to tell you before you left. I mean, you just found out about your dad and all.

Long pause.

I think we need to take a break.

A longer pause.

No, I can't drag this out. I'm moving out. I've put up with your stupid dreams long enough. You never finish anything, Grant, ever. You start something, it gets tough, you quit. We both know this music thing is just going to end up as another of your failures. You'll do it for a while, something will go wrong, or you'll get discouraged, and you'll be moving on to the next pipe dream. I want to be with somebody who's actually going somewhere in life. There are things I want and you can't give them to me. Anyway, I really am sorry to tell you this way. Hope things go okay in Virginia.

Grant ended the call and tossed his phone onto the passenger seat. He stared ahead, stunned as the trees zipped past on either side. Three years together and she couldn't even tell him to his face. What the hell? Maybe she was right. Perhaps a college degree and a safe career choice *would* be better for his future. He had a vision of himself trying to teach anthems to hormonal teenagers in a high school band and the very thought made him itch all over. He was a damned good musician and he *would* make it. Screw Suzanne. She'd be sorry when she saw him rocking out arenas. Besides, he'd loved his guitar a lot longer than he had loved her. But the coldness of her message shocked him. His GPS flickered and he cursed. He rapped on it twice before realizing what was really going on.

"You have got to be kidding me."

Blue lights flashed in his rear-view mirror and with them came the icy feeling in the pit of his stomach that always accompanied a traffic ticket. "Haven't seen a damn soul for miles and the first person I meet is a cop." Could this day get any worse? He hadn't been speeding but, with all the attention he'd been paying to his phone and GPS, he had doubtless had trouble staying on his side of the center line on the winding mountain road.

He scanned the roadside for a place to pull over but there was precious little space. The mountain rose up to his right at a steep incline and to his left fell away into a dark valley. The cop was riding his ass now, and cold sweat trickled down the back of Grant's neck as he wondered if the guy was getting impatient with him for not pulling over right away. What was he supposed to do? Stop in the middle of the road?

He was about do to that very thing when he spied a turn-off to his right. He winced as the encroaching shrubs scraped the paint job on his '68 Camaro. Finally far enough off the road to feel safe, he killed the engine and, careful not to make any sudden moves, took his wallet from his back pocket.

He turned to roll down the window and gasped, jerking involuntarily and dropping his wallet. A dark shaped loomed in the window, gleaming teeth bared. Heart pounding, he blinked and the image came into focus. A man in a beige uniform, mirrored shades, and a wide-brimmed hat. How had the cop gotten to Grant's car so fast?

Still grinning, the cop tapped the window with a yellow fingernail.

"Sorry," Grant called, cranking the handle for all he was worth, wishing for an automatic window. "I'm a little lost and I was trying to look at my..."

"Just get your license and hand it to me, son." The cop had a nasal voice with a touch of mountain twang, but his big hands and authoritative manner chased away any feelings Grant might have had of city superiority. His name tag read "J. Barton."

He handed over his license, proud that his hands weren't trembling. Biting his lip, he waited for a chance to explain himself and possibly ask for directions, but was hesitant to be the first to break the silence.

Barton held the license up. "Grant Shipman," he read aloud. He pursed his lips and tapped his chin. "You Andrew's boy?"

Grant's heart sank. "Yes, officer." His mouth was dry and his voice scratchy.

"Sheriff."

"Sorry, Sheriff. Yes, Andrew was my dad." He paused, searching Sheriff Barton's face to see if the admission had any obvious impact, but could see none. "I'm headed to the memorial service, but the road to Wallen's Gap isn't showing up on my GPS. I was trying to look at it and check my directions. I know I shouldn't do that when I'm driving."

"Damn shame about your daddy." Barton handed back Grant's license. "Damn shame. He was a good man."

"Thank you." There wasn't much else Grant could say. He and his father had never been close, and the elder Shipman had moved to Wallen's Gap a long time ago.

"You going to see to his affairs? His house and the like?"

"I suppose so. But not until after the funeral, of course." Grant grimaced. He didn't relish the thought of sorting through a dead man's possessions, especially a man whom he felt he should have known better, should have cared for more deeply.

"It's just a dirt road into town from this side of the mountains. You'd best follow me." Barton turned and strode back to his patrol car.

Grant sagged against the headrest, took a deep breath, and exhaled slowly. He had avoided a ticket and found himself a guide to town. Perhaps this day was about to get better.

Cassie took a deep breath and stepped into the community center beside the tiny Wallen's Gap supermarket. Her heart hammered and her nerves made her angry. She needed help and wouldn't let pride get in the way.

"Hello, Cassie." The gray-haired woman at the desk greeted her with a smile that was more genuine than her too-white dentures.

Cassie ground her teeth. Everyone knew everyone in this tiny craphole of a town. "Hello, Mrs. Golding."

A moment's uncomfortable silence hung in the air.

"You'd like to see the counselor?" Golding eventually asked, her voice gentle.

Cassie nodded, not quite able to meet the woman's eye.

Golding stood, favored Cassie with a kind smile, and stepped away down a corridor. Moments later she returned. "She's free. Second door on your left."

Cassie tried not to roll her eyes. The only counselor in a small town where half the people thought psychology to be just one of the many tools of the devil wasn't likely to have people beating down her door for appointments.

The woman in the office had a familiar face, but Cassie couldn't place her. "Cassie Brunswick, is it? I'm

Doctor Houghton. Please come in and sit down."

Cassie took the offered seat. Houghton. She'd gone to school with a Clare Houghton, but they had never been close. This must be Clare's mother. She took in her surroundings in a quick glance: a sofa and chair, a tiny bookshelf stuffed with self-help books, and a spartan, metal desk, neatly organized, above which hung a framed diploma from Stuart College. Two whole hours away! By Wallen's Gap standards, this woman was a world traveler. Cassie supposed she should get on with it before she changed her mind. "Everything we talk about is confidential, right?" she asked.

Houghton took a pad and pencil from her desk and sat in a chair opposite. "Yes, absolutely. You can be open and honest and nothing needs to ever leave this room. Unless I think you're about to commit a crime or harm yourself. That's not the case, I presume. Is it?"

Cassie shook her head and stared at her hands in her lap. She'd bitten her nails down to the quick. Her grandmother would have had a fit. The room seemed to press in on her as she searched for words. She had no idea where to start.

"It's all right," Houghton said softly. "Tell me what's on your mind."

"I've been seeing this boy, Carl." She stopped, unsure again.

"How old are you, Cassie?" There was no trace of judgment in the woman's tone.

"Just turned eighteen."

"Carl is twenty, isn't he?"

"Twenty going on twelve." How had she not seen what an immature jerk he was? She'd known from the start he was broken, but didn't count on just how badly.

Houghton nodded, and scribbled on her pad. "Take all the time you need."

"Well, it's just everything really." Inside, a floodgate opened. "He scares me and he's always getting wasted, he smokes so much weed, and has all these stupid ideas about stuff. I want to break up with him, but he says he couldn't live without me. And he says I need him too." She stopped, dragged a breath in, determined not to cry.

Houghton laid the pad on her knees. "Let me get this straight. You'd like to end things with Carl, but he makes you think you can't leave him?"

Cassie nodded.

"You can, you know. You can do anything you want."

Cassie made a derisive noise that was half-cough, half-snort. "Oh sure. Anything I want. Like what? I can't go anywhere. I can't get out of this stupid town. Besides, nobody would like it if I left him."

"What do you mean?" The counselor frowned.

"Never mind." Cassie gazed at the floor.

"Has he hurt you, Cassie?"

"No." Heat prickled the back of her neck and she felt the same old urge to defend the loser. Her loser.

"Have you two had sex?"

The boldness of the question shocked Cassie briefly, but she bit it down. "No. Well, not actual sex, no. I never have."

Houghton jotted something down. Cassie imagined the woman writing EIGHTEEN YEAR-OLD VIRGIN in big block letters and almost managed a smile.

"Has he pressured you about that?"

"Not exactly. It's kind of weird. He likes to, you know, fool around." Her cheeks burned at the admission. "But he doesn't push me to go farther. I don't want to anyway, but every guy, you know, wants to. It doesn't make sense. He acts like he doesn't want to go all the way with me, but he wants to own me or something. He *always* wants me to get him off. But never all the way. I don't really want to be with him, but when I start talking about us maybe taking a break, he gets so mad. I'm scared most of the time." The last bit came out in little more than a whisper and Cassie dropped her gaze to her clasped hands.

Houghton nodded, scribbled again on her pad. "You know, you don't have to be scared of him. You can..."

"I'm not just scared of him," Cassie interrupted.

"What else?"

Cassie paused, breathing deeply again. It was harder than she thought it would be to talk about the real problem. The real fear. "He says I sleepwalk." The word seemed so inadequate.

"Do you?"

"Maybe. He says I sleepwalk and he has to try to get me back into bed without freaking me out or anything. That's another thing that's been holding me back. Carl says if I leave him, who's going to look out for me at night then?"

"So you sleep together? Share a bed, I mean?"

Cassie nodded. She was still looking at her hands and couldn't see the woman's face, but she thought she registered a note of mild disapproval. Typical for this town. Just about every girl got initiated in the back seat of somebody's car during her freshman year, but as soon as they became parents themselves, you'd think they'd worn a chastity belt until they were thirty.

"I do sometimes. I usually stay at home, but I don't want to be there when Daddy gets really drunk, so I crash at Carl's."

"Do you sleepwalk at other times, when you're not at Carl's house?"

Cassie couldn't say anything, a lump of nerves sitting heavy in her throat like a cold rock.

"Cassie?" Houghton's attention was fully upon her now. The note pad lay forgotten on her lap.

"Sometimes I wake up and my feet are muddy. Once my nightshirt was all torn and there was blood on it."

Houghton shifted forward, elbows on her knees. "Blood?"

"I couldn't find any cuts or anything." Cassie bit her lip, not sure if she should say the rest. Then again, what was the point of seeing a counselor if she didn't spill her guts? She blurted the words out before she could change her mind. "I don't think it was my blood."

"Whose was it then?" Houghton articulated each word in careful, measured tones. The woman was trying too hard not to sound judgmental.

The tears started despite Cassie's best efforts. "I don't know."

Chapter 2

"Another book about the Templars. Big surprise." Grant tossed the volume into a box that already contained the works of Dan Brown plus a variety of fiction and non-fiction titles along the same theme. He'd sorted through roughly half of his dad's library. At first, he inspected each book carefully, even flipping through the pages in search of hidden cash or important documents, but an hour's futile efforts convinced him to give it up as a bad job.

The next book was a thick, heavy tome, cracked with age and the stamped gold letters on the spine faded. He held it up to the light and read the words aloud. "Demonology and The Bible."

Frowning, he flipped through the pages, trying to get a feel for the content. The title made it sound like a Christian book of some sort, but the contents put him to mind of a horror novel. He stopped at a black and white print showing a demon hunched over the supine body of a naked young woman who lay bound to an altar. He didn't know what unsettled him more: its rapacious expression or hers of terror. A shiver ran up his spine and he had the sudden urge to toss the book into the fireplace and burn it. The momentary irrationality passed and he put it in the box with the other religious books.

He'd hoped that, in the process of settling his father's affairs, he'd learn a little something about the man who had been an enigma to him for so long. So far, all he'd determined was his father loved his home in the mountains, his conspiracy thrillers, and apparently liked to read about religions, no matter how obscure. Or how sinister.

Grant stared into space as his thoughts drifted back to Suzanne. His stomach iced slightly at the thought of her packing up all her stuff and leaving. They had been together a long time. It was hard to imagine that she had just up and left like that. Then again, they'd been high school kids when they first started dating, and they'd had problems from the start. Everything he did stressed her out: his decision to drop out of college, his string of part-time jobs, his musical pursuits, his band practices, his seedy gigs. Meanwhile, she pursued corporate greatness, going to school year-round, earning her business degree after only three years, and recently accepting a boring, entry-level job at some faceless corporation in an equally faceless glass building. Come to think of it, he didn't know where she worked or what she did, aside from the fact that it involved a lot of bitching at the dinner table. He hadn't thought they were as doomed as she had suggested. Clearly he had been quite naïve there. Now he was all alone. *You never finish anything!* Her words haunted him.

Two razor sharp knocks on the door jolted him out of his emo moment and he grimaced as he stumbled to answer, awkwardly navigating the clutter he'd created in the spacious living area. Who could it be? He didn't know anyone and who, aside from the cop who'd stopped him, even knew he was here? He reached the knob and hesitated, visions of Deliverance-style hillbilly perverts flashing through his mind. He dismissed them with a rueful laugh and opened the door.

No one was there.

He cocked his head to the side like a confused dog and stepped out into the cool mountain air. There was no car in the driveway, save his own. He strode out onto the front porch and peered out into the woods. Nothing.

"Hello?" His voice sounded weak and tentative, so he summoned his inner thug and tried again. "Somebody fucking around out here?" That was better, though not by much. It suddenly occurred to him that anyone who was messing with him wouldn't answer back. In fact, whoever had knocked might be sneaking around back at this very instant. He stepped back inside, shut the door harder than necessary, locked it, and looked around for a weapon. His dad's Civil War era musket, complete with bayonet, hung above the fireplace. Nice. Now all he needed were cartridges, lead balls, and an inkling of how to load and fire the thing. He hurried into the kitchen area and, in a drawer full of tarnished silverware, found a carving knife with a long, triangular blade. It would have to do.

He moved to the back door and peered out the dirty window. If trees were out to get him, he was screwed, because that was all he saw in any direction. Clutching the knife, he opened the back door and moved out beneath the canopy of the forest that grew right up to the back edge of the house. He strained his eyes and ears, but neither saw nor heard anything. He was alone. It must have been a tree limb knocking against the side of the cabin. That or his imagination running wild.

There it was again. This time there was no question about the knock. He heard it clear as day. In a flash he was off, sprinting around the corner of the cabin. In the time it took to think, *At least I'm not running with scissors,* he was there.

And he was alone.

"No freaking way." He kicked at a loose rock and sent it bounding across the clearing in front of the cabin. The forest floor was carpeted in a thick layer of dry leaves. There was no way anyone could have run away that fast without him at least hearing them. He made a circuit of the cabin, looking for footprints but found exactly what he had expected--nothing. More unnerved than he cared to admit, he returned to the cabin and began gathering his things. He'd head to town, grab a cup of coffee and a bite to eat and clear his head. At the last second he grabbed the old demonology book that had caught his attention earlier. He didn't know why, but he suddenly wanted it out of the house, or maybe it wanted out, or something equally irrational. In any case, he shoved the book into his backpack.

He kept the knife too.

The interior of *Cup-of-Joe* was as grimy as its plate glass front window where chipped paint advertised the "Best Cup of Coffee in Town!" Faces turned toward Grant as he entered and all stared with mingled curiosity and disdain as he ordered and took a seat. Their conversations slowly started up again when he refused to meet any of those inquisitive eyes. *Fucking hick town,* he thought to himself. *If they were dogs, they'd all be sniffing my ass right now.* He'd be glad when the funeral was over and he could clear up and get out. Maybe he should just pile everything up in the woods and set it on fire, leave the cabin an empty shell, and get a real estate agent to sell it.

The thought had occurred to him that having a cabin in the country might be nice. He wasn't really the rural type, but he appreciated peace and quiet, nature, clear skies and fresh air. But this certainly didn't seem like the place for it. Maybe he'd sell out, take the proceeds and buy a little place somewhere else. Somewhere less... inbred.

The waitress put his coffee and eggs on the table and gave him a friendly, if distant, smile. "Anything else?"

He returned the smile, shook his head. "No, thanks." A thought occurred to him. "Say, did you know Andrew Shipman?"

The waitress's friendly face turned sad. "Sort of. Not really. My daddy knew him, from when they were in the lodge together. Terrible that he died. So young for a heart attack."

Grant nodded, now wondering why he'd asked. "Was he a... I dunno, was he a nice guy?"

"I guess so." She pursed her lips and cocked her head. It was a cute look for her. "Like I said, I didn't really know him, but he was always friendly, always had a grin on his face when he stopped in."

A part of Grant wished he knew his father better, but only a small part. The bastard walked out on Grant and his mother years ago and all the memories from before that were bad. Perhaps it was easy to feel guilty now the man was dead. Perhaps he needed some kind of closure, though he doubted he'd find it out here among the mountains and trees. He tried to imagine the old man as a regular member of the community. "You said he and your dad were in the lodge together? What lodge?"

The waitress giggled. "You know, the Freemasons." She made a face like she was imparting a great secret. "Secret societies and covert men's business."

Grant laughed and a man at the counter cleared his throat altogether too loudly. The waitress jumped and hurried away. Annoyed, Grant turned to look and the fellow stared at him with hard, dark eyes. He was a bear of a man, with a red and blue checked shirt stretched tight over bulging, muscular arms and a swollen beer gut. Grant held his eye for a few very uncomfortable seconds but the bear was obviously not planning to look away. More frustrated than ever with this backward community, Grant turned back to his food. He cursed his shaking hand as he forked up lukewarm eggs.

Keeping his attention away from the hicks, and determined not to give them the satisfaction of leaving right after his lunch, Grant ordered a coffee refill and sat back in the chair. To give himself something to do he pulled out the demonology book. Inside the front cover he found an inscription he hadn't noticed before:

Brother Andrew,
May the demons always be outside your circle.
In darkness and disorder,
Your Brothers and Sisters of Kaletherex.

Grant furrowed his brow. What the hell was Kaletherex? And if they called him Brother Andrew, was this a gift from the Freemasons the waitress had just mentioned? If so, what did "Brothers and Sisters" mean? In Grant's limited knowledge, the Freemasons were an all-boys club. A sick feeling rising in his gut, he thumbed through the pages, keeping his body between the leatherbound volume and the others in the diner. He didn't want them to see it, to know he had it. If it felt sinister to him, no telling what these hillbillies would make of it. He wondered what they would have made of his dad had they known about the old man's interest in demonology.

The door bell jingled as a young, pretty redhead came in. Her downcast gaze didn't conceal her red eyes and puffy face. Their eyes met and he flashed her a tight smile. She seemed surprised, gave the merest nod and hurried past. He watched her faint ghost reflected in the plate glass window as she ordered a coffee and took a seat at the table behind him.

She had a creamy complexion, full lips, and body that had not yet succumbed to the local fare of chicken-fried everything. In fact, she was the first person he'd seen in this town whose immediate forbearers, he could be certain, weren't closely related. Maybe this place wasn't all bad after all. Forget Suzanne. Maybe he'd fool around with a mountain girl while he was in town. He hadn't been with another girl since their Junior prom. Might as well get something good out of this trip.

But the thought of Suzanne dumping him so casually was still a knife in the gut. He turned his attention back to the book and continued to flip through, the pictures growing increasingly horrific. Hideous creatures did despicable things to terrified victims. He read occasional passages about true names, binding incantations, genealogy, as if these things were real. He didn't know jack about the Freemasons, but he was sure this book was not Masonic. Two pages turned at once under the weight of something between them and a yellowed photo slid out. Maybe a bookmark.

The picture showed three men in long robes, with heavy rope belts. Hoods sat piled on their shoulders as they smiled broadly at the camera, each with their hand on the hilt of a large knife, buried guard-deep in the carcass of a goat. Grant stared, horrified, at the grinning face of his father staring back. The man in the middle of the three had a large, heavy-looking medallion hanging low against his chest, the only difference between himself, Grant's father and the man on the other side.

A gasp broke Grant's reverie. He looked around to see the pretty redhead, hand before her mouth in shock, staring at the photo over his shoulder.

He laughed nervously, stuffing it back between the pages. "Just an old film still, I think," he said, sounding fake even to himself.

The girl jumped up and ran from the diner, half-eaten sandwich and full cup of coffee forgotten. The bell on the front door clattered as she banged through.

Grant sat frozen for a moment before sweeping his things back into his backpack, tossing a ten on the table, and running after her. As he left, he noticed the big man at the counter scowling with undisguised contempt. What was his problem?

The girl hurried down the street, almost running. Sure, the picture was creepy, but why cut and run like that? She glanced back, spotted him, and picked up her pace.

"Wait a minute!" Grant called, moving up behind her. "Excuse me," he said, putting a hand on her shoulder. "Are you okay?"

She jerked away, whirling about to face him. "Just stay away from me!" She backed away from him like he was a rabid dog.

Grant held his hands up in front of his shoulders, palms out. "Look, I didn't mean to scare you. It's just that you seemed really shocked by that picture."

At the mention of the photograph, she blanched. The girl said nothing, turned away and continued down the street.

"I'm really sorry," Grant called after her.

She didn't look back.

Chapter 3

The Wallen's Gap Public Library occupied the corner of Main and Oak like a homeless man begging for change. It might have been a nice place back in its heyday, but the peeling paint and crumbling mortar made Grant a little nervous about closing the door too hard when he stepped inside. Past the threshold, the familiar smell of dusty tomes calmed his jangled nerves. A faded poster of President Bush, the first one, greeted him with a sun-bleached smile and the words, "A Thousand Points of Light." Bush the Elder held a copy of either *The Sun Also Rises* or *The Sound and the Fury*--the poster was in such bad shape it was hard to tell.

"Can I help you?" The speaker was an elderly woman with a face like a Venetian blind and shockingly yellow hair. Her tone said she had little interest in assisting anyone. She stood behind a battered mahogany counter topped by a stack of romance novels. He wondered if she was reading or preparing to re-shelve them.

"Yes, I was wondering if you have a public computer I could use. With internet access," he added. No telling what sides came with your entrée and what was a-la-carte around here.

One of the folds on the woman's face puckered into a disapproving frown. "You have to have a member number to log on to the system."

"Okay, can I get a number?" He put on his most winning smile.

"You have to have a library card to get a member number."

"Great! Can I get a library card?"

"You have to fill out a form and show identification." Her voice was so dull and her expression so flat that he honestly couldn't tell if she was trying to give him a hard time or not.

"Okay," he said, working hard to keep his tone friendly, "where can I get a form?"

"You can download it from the website."

Cracks formed in his calm demeanor and the back of his neck prickled. He gritted his teeth and was formulating a suitable reply when the woman actually cracked a tiny smile. Had he uncovered actual humor in this town? Alert the media!

"Or you can get one from me." She slid a form across the counter and even provided a pen without being asked.

He completed the form and handed it back along with his driver's license.

"Shipman," she mused. "You any kin to Andrew Shipman?"

"My dad." He was afraid to say more. What if his dad had been as unsavory a character as the photograph seemed to indicate? No telling what his reputation had been in such a small town. But the sheriff had called Andrew a "good man." Grant didn't know what to think.

"Are you living in his place now?" Her tone and expression remained neutral.

Fearing some rule about not giving library cards to out-of-towners, he answered in the affirmative. A few minutes and a donation to the elementary school library later, he was the proud holder of a Wallen's Gap Library card. He stifled a guffaw when he saw his membership number was a whopping three digits long. Not too many readers around here.

The computer kiosk only held three units, but they were up-to-date and the internet connection crisp. He began with a simple web search:

Brothers and Sisters of Kaletherex

His shoulders sagged when he saw the results.

Your search- brothers and sisters of Kaletherex- did not match any documents

He tried "kaletherex" alone and in combination with "wallen's gap" but achieved no better results. He hated to admit failure so quickly. He considered for a few minutes, and a thought sprang to mind that sent a chill down his spine. He set his jaw and typed in "andrew shipman brother of kaletherex wallen's gap."

This time, he got a single hit. It was a cached document containing the phrase "Brother Andrew Shipman." No mention of Kaletherex, but it was something. He clicked the print icon and heard the whir of the printer... behind the front desk. Lovely.

He logged off and hurried over to the desk, taking out his wallet as he went. He wasn't sure why, but he didn't like the idea of the woman knowing what he was looking at. She handed the paper to him, her eyes passing only a quick glance across it before she handed it over. He thought he saw the ghost of a shadow pass over her face, but it could have been his imagination.

"Twenty cents, please." She held out a withered hand.

He handed her a dollar bill.

"I don't have change." She didn't sound the least bit apologetic. In fact, she looked affronted that he didn't have two dimes in his pocket.

"That's okay. You can owe me." He gave her his best conspiratorial smile, but she just stared at him. "Uh, keep the change. Thank you for your help." Duly cowed, he let her disapproving stare chase him out the front door.

Out on the street, he took a deep breath of mountain air. Foremost in his mind was a single thought. The red-haired girl in the diner had reacted to the picture of his dad. She knew something. He had to find her.

Reluctant to go back to the cabin early, Grant wandered around the block from the library. Across the way, a playground occupied a scrubby patch of grass and windblown dirt. He smiled as he caught a flash of red hair. Could he be that lucky? He stopped at a lamppost, acting as if he read the printed sheets in his hand while he covertly watched the redhead. It was definitely her, playing with two little girls who looked like twins in floral print dresses, their chestnut hair tied in bunches. They couldn't be more than four or five years old. The redhead pushed them on swings and chased them from one piece of play equipment to another. She looked to be having fun, but something about her demeanor made Grant a little sad.

He drew a deep breath, hoping he could talk to her rather than scare her off. He started across the road, forming what he hoped was a pleasant and friendly smile on his face. She saw him coming and scowled, glanced quickly to the twin girls and back again. She looked like a rabbit, cornered and ready to bolt.

"Hey," Grant called out, as casually as he could. "You're the girl from the diner, right? I'm Grant." He dared a broader smile, hoping it would work better on her than it had on the librarian. No such luck.

Her eyes narrowed. "Cassie." She seemed a little reluctant to give him even that single word.

"These your sisters?" he asked, still trying to be friendly but not pushy.

She shook her head. "My neighbor's girls. I baby-sit."

"We're not babies!" one of the twins said in high-pitched indignation. She folded her pudgy arms and tapped a foot in disapproval. Grant wondered where she'd picked that up.

"Of course you're not, sweetie. It's just a figure of speech." Cassie favored the girl with a smile and, for a moment, the weight lifted and it looked like the sun shone on her face. But only for a moment. She looked back to Grant, eyes wary. "You're Andrew's son." It wasn't a question.

He nodded. "You know him?"

She shrugged.

"I didn't really know him at all," Grant said. "He wasn't much of a dad. He left when I was little and never came around after that."

Cassie gave a half-smile. "I wish my dad would leave sometimes."

"Yeah?"

She clammed up again. Grant looked uncomfortably around the park, across the road to municipal buildings, along to the corner dominated by a tall brick building with a bright white facade. His roving eye paused as he caught sight of the square and compass motif. Block letters raised in the stonework read *MASONIC TEMPLE.*

"That's where they meet," Cassie said quietly, making him jump. She half-smiled again at his discomfort.

"They?" he asked.

"Loads of the men in town. Freemasons. They think they're some hot shit secret society or something. Losers."

"Your dad among them?"

She nodded. "And yours. Well, he was..."

"Yeah, I know. I found some of his stuff at the house. Just the men?"

Cassie frowned, scuffed her ragged sneaker in the dirt. "Yeah. Womenfolk not allowed apparently."

"Do the women have a society of their own?"

She barked a laugh. "Not unless you count gossiping after church or at the grocery store."

Silence descended again. Cassie watched the twins run and play. One of them swept past with a swish of dress and said, "We live next door to Cassie!"

"So I heard." Grant smiled at the little girl, momentarily charmed by the precociousness of youth.

"Right next door to the church!" the girl announced

seriously, like this was essential information.

Grant smiled. "That's nice."

"Run along and play," Cassie said, her voice a little hard.

Grant saw her expression was guarded. Perhaps she didn't like the girl blurting out where she lived. He decided to change the subject. "I'm sorry that picture bothered you earlier."

Cassie's face closed, like a shutter had come down. "It's nothing."

"Sure. But even so, sorry about that."

"I just didn't like it, that's all." She seemed spooked.

Grant felt bad for her, but clearly something else was happening here. She knew more than she was letting on. "Did you recognize any of the people in that photo?" he asked. "Besides my dad, I mean."

Cassie opened her mouth to speak and another voice cut across them.

"This guy bothering you, Cass?"

A tall, rangy guy, with greasy hair in a scruffy ponytail strolled up to them and laid an arm across Cassie's shoulders, a blatant act of ownership. She flinched ever so slightly at his touch. He wore a grubby, checked flannel shirt and jeans that looked as though they'd never been washed. Heavy, scuffed workboots made his feet look three sizes too big for his skinny legs. His eyes were red and droopy, his mouth a little slack.

Enjoy your lunchtime bong? Grant thought to himself, but chose not to say anything.

"No, he's not," Cassie said, looking at Grant. Her eyes seemed to hold a warning.

The newcomer was about Grant's age, maybe a year or two older than Cassie. "We were just having a chat about nothing," Grant said. "I'm new in town."

"That right?"

Grant nodded, unsure where to go from there. "My dad died recently. He was a local here."

"That right?" the stoner said again.

Grant couldn't repress a slight smile. *Such witty repartee!* He held out a hand. "I'm Grant. Grant Shipman."

The stoner's eyes narrowed. He shook hands, though without any real conviction. "Carl. You Andrew Shipman's boy? *He* died recently."

This guy was a real Sherlock Holmes. "That's right. Did you know my dad? I didn't know him well at all."

"You need to leave my girlfriend alone. C'mon, Cassie."

Cassie shook his arm off as he tried to turn her around. "Carl! I can't go anywhere, I'm watching the girls."

Carl seemed to find the situation suddenly difficult, his face twisting into a confused frown. Grant swiftly sized things up. If Carl felt like his authority was being tested, he looked the sort to react badly to it. Cassie couldn't go anywhere, so Grant would need to break the tension. He clenched a fist, tempted to break the tension by breaking this loser's nose, but bit it down. His temper was another thing that stressed Suzanne out.

"Anyway," he said quickly, "I'd better be off. Gotta lot of stuff to do up at my dad's old place. That's where I'm staying for now."

He gave Cassie a reassuring smile, sneered at Carl, and strode off across the scrubby park without waiting for a response. There was something very uncomfortable between those two and he didn't want to get Cassie in any kind of trouble. And if Carl was anything other than stupid, it was trouble. Frustrated, he headed back to where he'd parked his Camaro, wondering what kind of answer Cassie would have given about the photo if they hadn't been interrupted.

Chapter 4

A soft knock at the door rattled Grant from dark thoughts. He hesitated, then decided anyone who meant him ill probably wouldn't announce their presence so boldly. Then again, who could tell with these locals?

He drew back the curtain just far enough to peer outside. A woman of middle years stood on the doorstep holding a cardboard box packed with food. Silver streaked her blonde hair, and wrinkles creased her forehead and the corners of her eyes. She saw him and smiled.

"I'm so sorry to drop in unannounced like this," she said while the door was still opening, "but Andrew turned off his home phone years ago and we didn't know any other way to reach you." She bustled in like an expected guest, chattering as she headed to the kitchen. "I'm Mary Ann Stallard, Pastor Edwin's wife. The sheriff told us you were in town, and we wanted to make sure you were welcome. Have you had supper yet?"

Grant caught a whiff of fried chicken and his stomach answered the question for him.

"You just have a seat then." Mary Ann pulled out a chair for him and started unloading her box. Grant sat down and watched, a little uncomfortably, as she laid out fried chicken, mashed potatoes, gravy, biscuits, green beans, corn, and a jar of sweet tea. In typical southern fashion, she apologized profusely for what she claimed was meager fare.

"It looks delicious. I can't remember the last time I had real home cooking."

"Well, you just enjoy yourself then. I'm going to take a little walk." She patted him on the shoulder and turned toward the front door.

"Do you want to join me?" Grant asked. "I doubt I can eat all this by myself." He didn't relish the thought of making small talk with his unexpected visitor, but it would have been rude not to offer.

"I'll be fine." She gave his shoulder a reassuring pat. "Take your time."

When the front door closed behind her, he chuckled and set to his meal. The chicken was the best he'd ever had-- crispy on the outside and juicy on the inside. The biscuits were perfect, and the green beans and corn were fresh, though seasoned with a little too much salt and bacon grease for his liking. He could almost feel his arteries clogging with every delicious bite. By the time Mary Ann returned, he was working on his second plate. She nodded in approval and started wandering around the living room.

Grant did his best to ignore her as she hovered about, looking in turn at the paintings on the wall and his dad's old musket. As he stuffed the last bite of biscuit and gravy in his mouth, he noticed her kneeling beside the boxes where he'd been sorting his dad's books. Her back arched strangely, her fingers curled like claws, the nails jet black and far too long. Her face seemed stretched back, drawn tight and angular across her skull. She seemed to be growling deep in her chest. Grant gasped, his chair scraping back as he stood.

Mary Ann turned, her soft, middle-aged face curious, her hands resting on the edge of a box. Grant shook his head, blinked. What the hell was that? He swallowed, took a swig of tea, and cleared his throat.

"Did you want to borrow a book?" He kept his tone easy. "Dad had plenty of them. I figured I'd donate them to the library. I'm more of an e-book guy myself." He wondered if she even knew what an e-book was.

"Oh, no." The smile that suddenly spread across her face was so unlike her expression moments before that he found the change unsettling. "My husband lent your daddy a book. It isn't valuable, but it belonged to Edwin's great grandfather, and he'd love to have it back in his library." She rose unsteadily to her feet.

Cold suspicion trickled down his spine. "What was the title?"

"Oh, it didn't even have a title. Just a wrinkled old leather cover, kind of light brown in color. The pages are old and wavy and the words aren't even English. It's just a curiosity that was passed down through the family."

He relaxed a little. He'd assumed she was referring to *Demonology and The Bible*.

"Sorry, but I definitely haven't seen anything like that, and I've been through all the books."

"Are there any in the back rooms?" she asked. "I could go check for you."

Grant shook his head. "Nope, I've checked every nook and cranny, but I'll definitely let you know if it turns up."

Her face tightened and, for a moment, he thought she would protest, but she nodded. "Thank you kindly. I'll leave you our number, but you can find us at the parsonage. It's right by the church, and somebody's most always home."

She insisted he keep all the food he had not eaten, telling him he could return the dishes any time he liked. He thanked her and promised again to keep an eye out for the book. He stood in the doorway as she drove away, and didn't go back inside until her taillights vanished in the darkness.

He supposed her hospitality should warm his heart, but he felt cold inside. There was something wrong about this town.

A freaking iron key. That was the only thing his dad had left in his safe deposit box at the First National Bank of Wallen's Gap. Grant wondered why he'd even bothered to make the trip into town, enduring another round of dull stares and angry mutters from the local fauna. He'd kept an eye out for Cassie, but hadn't seen her. He was still convinced she knew something about his dad. Maybe she even knew something about the book the pastor's wife had been so interested in finding.

He'd searched every inch of the cabin, including the attic and the crawlspace, and was satisfied there was no lock the iron key would fit. He now stood on the front porch, twirling the key around his finger and thinking. Why put a key in a safe deposit box? The reasons were obvious. While the key itself might not have any intrinsic value, it must unlock something that did. His dad was keeping the key safe, keeping it away from someone else, or both.

Slapping his palm with the cold iron, he looked around. There was nothing out front except an old dog house, its roof sagging like an aged horse. He stepped down off the porch and circled the house. On the back side, the land sloped upward toward the peak of Clay Mountain far above. The pine forest that covered the mountainside was fast encroaching, casting the land in a dull hue of dark green. As Grant gazed up the hill, he caught a glimpse of weathered, gray wood. He climbed up the slope, heading directly toward it, nervous energy buoying his steps. Something told him he'd found what he was looking for.

An old smokehouse stood almost completely hidden in a dense stand of blackberry vines. He tried to push a few aside and got a handful of briars for his trouble. This wasn't going to be easy. He headed back to the house and returned a few minutes later with an old sickle. Its curved blade was pitted with rust and the edge was dull, but it would have to do.

For half an hour he hacked away at the tangled vines. His hands and forearms were scraped and bloodied and his muscles burned, but he felt good. He hadn't had a proper workout since he'd left home, and it was nice to work up a sweat. When at last he'd cleared a path to the smokehouse door, he tossed the sickle aside and withdrew the key from his pocket.

His heart sank. The door was secured by a simple padlock. Whatever lock the iron key opened, this wasn't it. He'd worked for nothing.

"What the hell?" he said to no one in particular. "Might as well see what's in here." He picked up a rock and took out his frustrations on the padlock until it snapped off. He put his hand to the door but, as he was about to open it, a cool breeze passed over him. He paused, gooseflesh rising up on his arms. Where had that breath of air come from in the midst of this dead, calm forest? Puzzled and a little spooked, he retrieved the sickle, holding it in a white knuckled grip, and pushed the door open.

Grant tested the floorboards before stepping inside. The smokehouse was dark, dusty, and filled with cobwebs. Thin shafts of light pierced the cracks in the rough-hewn walls, shining on heaps of mouldering burlap sacks. A coil of rope hung from a hook on one of the overhead beams.

"Shit." He kicked a pile of burlap, sending up a cloud of dust that burned his eyes and set him to coughing. When the dust cleared, he looked down and his eyes fell on a small door set in the base of the wall. The keyhole in the center looked like the perfect fit. For no particular reason, he looked around to see if anyone was watching. He knelt, inserted the key in the lock, and turned it.

The door swung open, revealing a small, recessed area carved into the natural rock that abutted the smokehouse. Inside lay a book. The cover was a light tan, creased leather, strangely soft to the touch. The pages were heavy, rough-edged and covered in a curling, crabbed script that made Grant frown as he flicked through. Fascinated, he sat on a pile of mouldering burlap and turned to the front of the book, reading by a shaft of light through a gap in the wall behind him.

An inscription was written by hand inside the front cover, in a different language to the rest of the book. It used the alphabet as he knew it, though still not English. One word was clear, however - *Kaletherex*. He turned the page and realized the rest of the book was hand-written too, in a dark, reddish brown ink. A crooked smile tugged at one side of his mouth as he wondered if the thing was written in blood, but the smile faded like sunlight behind a passing cloud when it occurred to him that he might be right. A weird leather-bound book, written in blood, in an arcane, indecipherable script. "What the..?" His voice was barely a whisper.

As if in answer, the cold breeze blew again, shifting the edges of the sacking all around, chilling him. The breeze seemed to carry a voice, *read read read*, like a distant echo.

Grant jumped up, looked around. "Who's there?"

He stood still for close to a minute, listening so hard he felt as though his ears must be standing out on the sides of his head. Nothing but the susurration of the leaves and pine needles outside, the occasional call of a bird. He stuck his head out the door of the smokehouse and saw nothing but trees.

Losing my freaking mind. He sat down again.

The pages were heavy, thick, slightly waxy. He turned slowly through the book, examining each page in turn. He could make no more sense of it than if he had been trying to read Chinese or ancient Greek, but there was something compelling about the shapes and ellipses of the text. His eyes moved slowly, sliding around the words and paragraphs. This had to be something important, something worth locking in a safe carved into bedrock. The key to which was kept far away in a strong box in the bank. Was it something so valuable it needed security? Or something else. Important? Dangerous?

He turned another page and jumped, a small gasp escaping his lips. Across the double page spread was a drawing in exquisite detail, fine lines and smooth shading. It showed a young, naked girl on a table, her arms and legs strapped wide to make an X of her body. There were marks on her skin, spirals over her heart, stomach and forehead. Candles stood around her on the table's edges and strange symbols, similar to the text of the book, were carved into the wooden tabletop. Several figures stood around her holding a variety of implements: knives, scythes, branches of gnarled wood. One held a dripping organ, like the liver of a sheep or cow... or something. It looked too large to be human.

The girl's head was tipped back, her mouth wide in a scream, eyes squeezed shut. Grant held the book up closer to his eyes, fascinated by the gruesome detail. He could see where the straps at her ankles and wrists bit into the skin, rubbed it raw as she pulled against them, could see tears and sweat on her face. As his eyes narrowed in morbid fascination, the picture moved, the girl thrashed and screamed, the sound pierced his ears. A chant rose up from the people gathered around her, candles flickered, somewhere a sonorous drum beat a solid, regular dirge.

With a cry, Grant dropped the book and staggered back, tripped against a pile of sacking and sat heavily. His heart pounded as he struggled to recover his breath.

"What's going on in there?" a sharp voice called from outside.

Grant shuddered, adrenaline coursing through his body like an electric shock. He scooped the book from the floor, shoved it back in the rock safe and locked the door. He shoved sacking up against the door to hide it and pocketed the key as he turned and stepped out of the smokehouse. Three young men stood a few yards down the path, grizzled and a little dirty. They looked at him with hooded, suspicious eyes.

"You all right?" the gangly fellow in the middle of the three asked.

Grant forced a smile, tried to ignore his still hammering heart. "Yes, fine."

"Thought we heard you holler."

"Just tripped in the dark and banged my elbow. Wasn't watching where I was going." He rubbed one elbow for emphasis, not even believing himself.

"What's in there, anyhow?" The young man stepped toward the smokehouse, his grin not quite friendly.

Grant made a dismissive gesture. "Nothing at all, just old burlap and some broken shelves. I had to break the padlock off to get in because I couldn't find the key. I was hoping there might be something interesting in there, but there's nothing." He stopped, realizing he was rambling like a fool, and shrugged.

"Mm hmm," the man said.

An uncomfortable silence hung in the air for a few seconds as they looked at each other. Finally, Grant said, "So, can I help you?"

"Wondered if *we* might help *you*. I'm Jed, this is Cliff and Jesse." He indicated the others with a quick gesture. "We're Pastor Edwin's boys. Mama said we ought to come on up here and lend you a hand,."

Grant chose not to mention it was a long trip to lend a hand unasked for. "I'm not really sure there's anything you can help me with. Thanks anyway."

"You don't need no stuff cleared out or anything moved? You can't haul much in that car of yours. We got us a truck back there."

Grant forced another smile. "Well, I do appreciate that. But I'm not ready to move anything yet. There's still a bunch of stuff to go through. When I am ready to start throwing things out, I could certainly use a truck and some extra hands though."

Jed nodded. "Well, you be sure and give us a holler then."

"I will, thanks."

Discomfort swelled in the air as nobody moved. Grant felt trapped in the door of the smokehouse, pinned by the strangely unfriendly gaze of the three men who claimed to be there to help him. He looked from one to the next and back again, desperately trying to think of something to say. He eventually gestured back down towards the house. "I should be..."

Jed spoke over him immediately, like he had been waiting for Grant to speak, purely so he could interrupt. "Well, we'll be off then."

Grant nodded. "Right. Sure. Thanks again."

"Uh huh."

They didn't move, or even blink. Grant felt a kind of pressure building up that made him both incredibly uneasy and frustrated. Trembling set in, making his hands shudder slightly at his sides. Unspoken violence hung in the air between them like a storm cloud. He felt his fists closing of their own accord, and realized he had to say or do something. He opened his mouth to speak and Jed and his brothers instantly turned and ambled slowly off back down the path without another word. Grant stood, shivering, in the doorway of the smokehouse until he heard their truck rumble into life and fade off down the mountain.

Chapter 5

It was the same dream again. Cassie lay bound on a table, candlelight flickering across her naked body. Ghostly figures circled her, chanting in low tones. She never quite knew what they were saying. The words seemed to dangle there just beyond the edge of comprehension. Somewhere a drum pounded out a slow, deep, relentless beat.

She thrashed about, trying to free herself, but the bonds held tight. Her breath came in gasps, drowning out the drone of the pale figures that drew ever closer. She wanted to pull away, but how did one do that when they were all around you?

The figures never touched her in the dreams, but the words seemed to. It was as if the sounds had substance, and as the chanting reached a crescendo, she felt cold, dry hands caress her. She pressed her knees together and tried to pull her legs up as the invisible hands traced the curves of her flesh, moving ever downward, but her bonds held fast. A stray tear trickled down her cheek as one of the figures leaned in close and, for the first time, she recognized a face.

She started awake, sweat pouring down her face and soaking her pillow. Her t-shirt clung tightly to her. She looked around her bedroom, taking in the cheap paneling, the secondhand lamp, and the dollar store kitsch, reassuring herself that, once again, it had been a dream. Out of habit, she checked her wrists for chafing, but they were fine.

The chafing had only happened once, the first time she'd had the dream. That had been the one and only time she'd let Carl talk her into smoking with him. He'd assured her it was weed, but he must have added something to it because she almost immediately lost consciousness, suffered through the first of these awful nightmares, and awoke in her bed hours later. Carl said she'd gotten sick and he'd taken her home, but she'd been so freaked out she'd driven two hours to the E.R. in Kingsville to get a rape exam. The results had been negative. That had been a relief, but it still left the chafing around her wrists and ankles. He might not have raped her, but he sure as hell had drugged her, tied her up, and done something perverted. No other explanation made sense.

After that, she'd tried to break things off with him, but he wouldn't listen. He kept coming around as if nothing had happened. Stranger still, everyone in town assured her that Carl was a good boy and just needed her to set him straight. Why the population of Wallen's Gap seemed to have a stake in their relationship was beyond her. Between Carl's persistence, or arrogance, and the not-so-gentle prodding of every adult in her life, she'd finally given in. Why couldn't she stand up for herself? That counselor lady had been no help at all. Life in Wallen's Gap was like living in a fish bowl. Everyone knew too much about her business.

That wasn't entirely true. There was the new guy, Andrew Shipman's son. What was his name? Grant? He'd been looking at that awful book...

And then her stomach lurched and she felt suddenly dizzy. Memories of the dream returned and she remembered the face she'd recognized.

"I need to talk to Grant Shipman," she whispered to herself. She glanced at the digital alarm clock beside her bed. It was only 11:30. Late, but not too awful late if she hurried. From the next room, Daddy's drunken snores told her he wouldn't wake before morning.

She slipped into jeans, flip flops, and a hooded sweatshirt, grabbed her purse and keys, and tiptoed down the hall and out the front door. The cool night air calmed her nerves, but she felt vulnerable out in the dark. The waxing moon afforded enough light to see that Daddy had parked his truck on the street and didn't block her in like he so often did when he tried to keep her home.

She slipped into her beat up Honda Accord, which she always parked facing downhill for occasions such as this, put it in neutral, and coasted down the road. When she was well away from home, she fired up the engine, flipped on the headlights, and headed for the Shipman cabin.

As she drove, she thought about what she would say to Grant. *Hi there, I've been dreaming about your daddy stripping me naked and tying me to a table.* That would go over well. It didn't matter. She'd tell him the truth and trust him to understand. Her thoughts returned to the book she'd seen him reading in the diner. She hadn't realized it then, but there was something about it that reminded her of the dreams. Maybe she would find the answer.

The Shipman place lay at the end of a narrow dirt road that wound through a hollow at the foot of Clay Mountain. Last time she'd gone up here was two years ago with a boy from school, but she'd lost her nerve when his hands wandered too far. She hadn't been back since, but the way remained familiar. Things didn't change much in Wallen's Gap.

She rounded a curve and had to slam on the brakes to avoid hitting an old Ford F-250 that was blocking the road. The Honda skidded to a halt inches from the truck, sending up a cloud of dust.

"What in the holy name of Jesus?" Who would park their truck sideways across the road? There couldn't be more than two feet on a side to spare. She looked up at the empty cab. Whoever it was had abandoned the vehicle. Where had they gone? The dark thoughts in her mind manufactured all kinds of deadly scenarios. Had something happened to them.

Someone rapped on her window and she shrieked in fright.

"Sorry bout that, Cass. I didn't mean to scare you."

She turned to see Cliff Stallard leaning down to look through her window, his bulk straining the buttons of his faded chambray shirt. His grin said he was anything but sorry.

"Why are you blocking the road?" She managed to put some heat into her words despite the fright he had given her.

"Run out of gas. Saw I was on fumes, tried to turn around, and, wouldn't you know it? Died right here in the middle of the road." He paused. "What are *you* doing up here?"

"Oh. I needed to talk to Grant."

"Grant, is it? You already know him so good that you come see him in the middle of the night?" He leered, his tobacco-stained teeth gray in the dim light. "That ain't a good idea, Cass. What if people found out?"

"No, it's not like that." She was suddenly flustered. Even at midnight she couldn't get a modicum of privacy in this town.

"Daddy's gonna be here in a few minutes to bring me some gas. I think it would be a good idea if you was gone when he gets here, him being the pastor and all."

Cassie looked again at the big truck blocking the way, and nodded. "I suppose you're right." She turned the Honda around and headed back down the road, shame and impotent rage welling inside her. She wasn't going to give up. She had to find out the truth, and she believed Grant held the key.

At the end of the dirt road, Clay Mountain silhouetted like a sleeping giant behind her, she paused. Where the dirt met the tarmac there was nothing but trees to left and right. But on the opposite side of the road, about fifty yards to the left, was a turnoff. One of those places for people to pull over and rest if they were too tired to continue on their journey or something.

Cassie drove to it, pulled up close to the trees and parked in deep shadow. She killed her engine and lights and sat there, waiting. Why had Cliff been up at the Shipman cabin? And who runs out of gas like that, halfway through a three-point turn? Ten minutes passed, then twenty, and still no sign of Pastor Edwin and the gas he was supposed to be bringing. It shouldn't take this long. After thirty minutes, Cassie's nerves began to jangle like a cold hand creeping up her spine. She thought about walking through the woods to get up to the cabin, but that was a long way and she was likely to get lost.

After forty five minutes her nerves got the better of her and she was about to start up the car and go home when headlights lit the distance, coming from Wallen's Gap. The lights blinded her as they swelled up, painting the trees in bight greens, before zooming straight past the turnoff to Grant's cabin and barrelling on down the road. Cassie let out a breath she'd been unaware she was holding and fired up the battered Honda to head back home. Something very strange was happening and it scared her to think what it might be.

Chapter 6

Grant sat hunched over a steaming cup of coffee, scowling. It wasn't the coffee that had him in a foul mood. In fact, that was the only good thing about the day so far. But he was tired, annoyed and, if he was honest, more than a little scared. He'd endured a terrible night's sleep, his dreams plagued with screaming girls tied to tables, and strange rednecks with faces that kept morphing into twisted, demonic visages as he tried to escape from them along darkened corridors, his legs like lead. Several times during the night he had woken himself crying out, the sensation of pursuit still fresh in his adrenalized, sweating body.

Eventually he dragged himself from bed and brewed coffee, resigned to the fact that he would get no more rest anyway. He had an appointment in Kingsville at ten a.m. to sign off on a bunch of legal paperwork and figured he might as well get an early start. It wasn't like there would be much in the way of traffic, but he had to somehow justify his rising close to dawn.

Grant finished his coffee and chewed his way through toast that tasted like cardboard and sawdust on his tongue, then gathered the papers he needed. Two hours on his cell phone the afternoon before and several more hours through the evening had finally revealed that he needed to go to his father's attorney in Kingsville and then find a notary and the county courthouse, to file the numerous, frustrating forms. At least once this was done, he would have nothing left to worry about but his father's personal possessions and cabin. A part of him was tempted once again to just give up on it, keep driving once he was finished in Kingsville and have a real estate agent deal with selling the cabin and everything in it. Did he really need the hassle of all this garbage and these hillbillies? But with Suzanne gone, what did he have to go back to? An apartment as empty and pointless as this cabin.

His eyes roved the spare furnishings and something like nostalgia drifted over him. He had not known his father well, but he felt there was a certain closure to be found here. He owed it to himself and his dad to make the right decisions with all this. And besides, he might turn up something valuable or personal that he could treasure. Some connection to the man. The train of thought led Grant back to the strange book in the smokehouse and he shook his head, clearing his thoughts quickly before he ruminated on that too much. It made him intensely uncomfortable to even picture it in his mind's eye. He had seen that picture move, heard the girl's scream and the chant and the drum.

"The hell with this," he muttered, forcing the thoughts from his mind. He grabbed his keys and left as the soft pink of dawn began to give way to the blue of a clear, bright day.

As he climbed into his car the sensation of being watched washed over him, prickled up his spine and gently gripped the back of neck. Why did this keep happening? Half in the car door, he paused, looked around. Trees shifted in a soft breeze, birds sang. No person anywhere to be seen. He walked away from the car a few paces and looked deeper into the forest, down the driveway, up towards the smokehouse.

"Anyone there?" he called out. "I'm about to leave for the day, so if you need to talk to me, now's the time!"

He felt like a fool calling out to the woods. His heart hammered ridiculously fast, but no one answered. He didn't know what he would have done had anyone actually replied. Probably jump right out of his shoes. With an annoyed grunt, he climbed into the car and turned the key. The sound of another engine barked and rattled over his own the moment his fired. With a curse, he killed his again. The distant sound of a diesel motor drifted through the air. He opened the car door and hopped up on the hood, peering down where the drive wound through the forest. The diesel sound was almost gone, receding down the dirt road leading away from the cabin. He caught a glimpse of a truck snaking through the twisting mountain road before it vanished down the hollow.

"What the fuck?" He slipped back into the car, restarted it and roared around in a wide U, spraying gravel up against the front of the cabin. With no regard for his shocks, he hammered down the rutted drive to where it met the paved road and skidded to a halt at the intersection. Nothing. No vehicle in either direction until the road curved away through the trees.

Maybe he had been hearing things. Hardly any sleep, his nerves in tatters, perhaps it had only been his own engine echoing through the forest. Was that even possible? But he'd seen the truck! Regardless, there was nothing to see now. He turned towards Wallen's Gap and was soon cruising through the main street.

Even this early there were people moving about, a smattering of cars gliding slowly by. He caught sight of a young girl, maybe sixteen, weirdly out of place in old-fashioned clothes, standing on a street corner as he passed. Her bonnet half-shaded her face, but her expression held such a deep and terrible sadness that Grant hit the brakes, twisting in his seat to look back. The girl was nowhere to be seen. He stared at the empty pavement where she had stood. She had definitely been standing right there. He ground his teeth. This fucking town.

Impotently angry at just about everything, he revved the engine and drove on. A block further, a flash of jeans and a white shirt caught his eye as he passed the park. Was that Cassie or was he seeing things again? Rather than risk a wreck, he hung a right, went around the block, and cruised by the park again. It was her. She sat alone on a swing, gently swaying back and forth, head down. Her hair obscured her face, but she seemed sullen, sad.

Grant pulled up to the curb, wound down the window. "Hey, Cassie!"

She looked up with a start, dragged one forearm across her face. "Oh, hi." Her voice was tight.

Grant frowned. Had she been crying? "Everything okay?"

She nodded, forced a smile that was totally unconvincing. "Sure, everything's good." She glanced left and right, almost as if she was afraid to be seen talking to him.

"You're up bright and early," he said with what he hoped was a reassuring smile.

Her shoulders hitched and dropped.

"You usually up so early?" He felt like a fool the moment the words left his mouth. What kind of lame ass thing was that to ask someone, especially a cute girl? As her face creased in a frown he hurried on. "I'm not. I hate early mornings as a rule. But I have to go to Kingsville today. Got to deal with some stuff about my dad."

Cassie's face slipped through a few quick changes of expression, surprise to thoughtfulness to something like hope. She nodded again. "Long drive," she said.

"Not as the crow flies but, with these winding roads, I figure a couple of hours, right?" There was suddenly something unsaid hanging in the air between them.

"About that," Cassie said. "You know, I..." She thought better of it, stopped abruptly.

Grant's heart did a two-step with nerves and he took a leap. "You need anything in Kingsville? I'd be happy to pick something up for you." Her eyebrows lifted, lips parted like she wanted to say something. "Or I could, you know, I could give you ride up there if you need it." Was he being a complete douche? Who offered such a long ride to someone they hardly knew?

Cassie looked around again, furtively. She chewed at her lower lip for a moment, clearly trying to come to some decision. "Actually, yeah, that would be really good. I do need to do something in Kingsville and I hate making that drive on my own."

Grant grinned, pleased with himself. Maybe there was something worthwhile in Wallen's Gap after all. He couldn't believe this cute girl had just agreed to a two hour each way trip with him. Suzanne's angry face flitted through his mind and he pushed the thought away. She had left him, so he had no time for guilt. He gestured with his head towards the passenger side. "Great. Hop in."

She hurried over and slipped into the seat beside him. "Thanks, this is nice of you," she said with a tight smile. "I don't want to be any trouble."

"No problem. Do we need to swing by your place to pick anything up?"

"No, let's just get going, okay?"

Grant's elation waned at her tense nervousness. She seemed strangely agitated. "Sure thing," he said, trying to keep his voice light and casual.

He pulled away from the curb, wondering what else he could say to ease her tension. As he made the turn up towards the highway he glanced in the rearview mirror and saw the tall, gangly boyfriend, Carl, standing outside the still closed hardware store, staring after them. Carl did not look happy at all.

Chapter 7

Cassie's heart raced as Grant gunned the engine and they left Wallen's Gap and Carl behind. Carl was going to be mad. She looked down at a hole in the thigh of her jeans and plucked absently at the thread, trying to decide where to begin. Now that she was alone with Grant, she couldn't seem to summon the courage to be honest with him. From the corner of her eye she saw him looking at her. She told herself not to blush, but she could feel her cheeks heating. He was cute, and not at all like the losers who populated her town.

"Can I say something?" Grant broke the silence so suddenly that she jumped. "About your boyfriend or whoever he is to you?"

Cassie nodded, not eager to hear whatever he had to say. She knew she should dump Carl, and her inability to do so embarrassed her. He was like an unsightly blemish.

"I've tried to be cool because I don't want to cause trouble for you. But I'm tired, and I'm fed up with the creepy ass people in Wallen's Gap, and if he steps to me the wrong way, or lays a hand on you where I can see him, I'm going to beat his ass."

Now she did look directly at him. She saw resolve in his eyes and, when he directed his gaze back toward the road, looked him up and down. Cassie almost felt like she was at a livestock show as she sized him up. He wasn't bulky, like Cliff Stallard, but he was tall and lean with whipcord muscles. He looked like he could handle himself.

"Why are you telling me? I'm not the one you want to beat up."

"In case it's going to cause a problem between you and Carl. You could..." He cleared his throat. "If you needed somewhere safe to go, you could stay at my dad's place. I guess it's my place now. I've got room."

"There's already plenty of problems between me and Carl. Your fists won't make it better or worse. Besides, he wouldn't fight you. It's the Stallards you need to worry about. Those boys love to brawl, and they don't fight fair."

"I met those three yesterday afternoon. They dropped by the cabin, claiming they wanted to see if I needed any help, but they were up to something. It was weird. I could almost hear the banjos playing in the background."

She giggled and he laughed too.

"Do you think all their ancestors were brother and sister, or just the last few generations?"

"Hey now!" she protested, still laughing. "We're not all inbred hillbillies, you know."

"Just the Stallards."

"Right." The moment was gone as soon as it had come, and they lapsed back into silence. Then something Grant had said rang a bell. "Hold on. You said the Stallard boys came by your place yesterday afternoon?"

"Yep."

"Cliff Stallard was back up there late last night. He said he was driving around and ran out of gas."

Grant snapped his head around and gave her a sharp look. "What does he drive?" She described the truck and Grant spat a curse. "He was still there this morning. When I went to leave, somebody cranked up a truck and drove away. I only caught a glimpse, but it's got to be him."

Cassie didn't know what to say. Clearly, Cliff had stayed there all night for some odd reason. What was he doing? Keeping people away, or keeping Grant in?

"Wait a minute." Grant arched an eyebrow. "How do you know he was at my place late last night?"

There it was. Cassie might as well tell him the truth.

"I came up there to talk to you, and he turned me away. I wanted to ask you about the book."

Grant flinched and his face went ashen. "You know about the book?"

"I saw you reading it at the *Cup of Joe*, remember?"

Grant's features relaxed. "Yeah, sure. What about it?"

Cassie wasn't buying it. She could tell when someone was hiding something. Perhaps it came from her childhood, when her daddy was still bothering to try to hide his drinking from her mother. Or perhaps it came from dating guys like Carl, for whom deceit was so ingrained in their character they no longer knew how to tell the truth. In any case, Grant wasn't being honest with her.

"What book did you think I meant?"

"What?"

"I want to play poker with you sometime. I'd have your money, your car, and every stitch of your clothes, cause you can't lie for shit."

"That last part sounded pretty good. Maybe later on

tonight? I think I saw a deck of cards in the cabin." He was trying to keep things light, but she could tell he was rattled.

"You've got a secret, Grant Shipman." She swallowed hard. "And so do I. I've got nobody else I can trust, so how about we both come clean, and maybe we can help each other?"

She watched as he chewed on that for a minute, his jaw working and his grip tightening and relaxing on the wheel. Finally, he nodded.

"Okay, but not here. After the attorney's office, we'll find somewhere quiet and I'll tell you everything."

Grant left the attorney's office and made his way to the cafe he and Cassie had agreed on. He felt marginally better about his father's affairs now that everything official was taken care of or in process. Red tape and bureaucracy were infuriating, but better than the worry of leaving something unfinished or some obscure law unheeded. Cassie sat in a window booth, staring worriedly across the street, playing with the straw in a big, empty milkshake glass. She looked the other way, hadn't seen him yet as he stood across the street. She was cute, but troubled. A part of him really wanted to get to know her better, but another part, maybe his sane side, screamed at him to pack up his father's stuff and get the hell out of this redneck, backwater hole.

Cassie tipped her head to one side and brushed a hand across her cheek. Was she crying? His desire to run away turned quickly to shame. This was a hole, but she was stuck here too, through no desire of her own. Cute or not, she needed his help. And, if he was honest, he needed hers. Perhaps she could help him learn more about his dad.

He crossed the street, making sure she would notice him coming and have a chance to gather herself.

"Hey," he said simply as he entered the booth, sat down opposite her.

She gave him a broad smile that didn't reach her eyes. "Hey yourself."

The waitress came over, took Grant's order of coffee, and raised an eyebrow at Cassie.

She shook her head. "That's all, thanks."

The waitress gave them a wink and a knowing smile as she left.

Grant laughed. "Awkward."

"Let 'em think whatever they like." Cassie grinned and raised her eyebrows.

"I like that attitude." And he did. Too often, she seemed beaten down, cowed even. When she showed a little spirit she was radiant.

They sat in silence for a while, Grant sipping his coffee, Cassie playing with her straw.

Eventually, Grant said, "So. Wanna tell me what's up?"

"Nice." She smirked at him. "You make me go first? Some gentleman you are."

"Okay, fine." He raised both hands in mock surrender. "I found a creepy fucking book that looks like it's written in blood and bound in human skin, and while I was looking at it the pages came alive and moved and screamed."

Cassie sat back in her seat, wide-eyed. He saw the panic in her, a trembling like a deer as it froze, trying to decide which way to bolt.

"You asked," he said, before she could hightail it out of there. "And I'm pretty sure those Stallard boys are after the damn thing. Their mom came by, acting all neighborly with food and chit-chat while she stalked around the cabin looking for something. Didn't even try to hide it. Then she sent those idiot sons of hers around."

"And you think they want the book?" Cassie's voice was tissue-paper thin.

"Obviously. I don't know if there's anything else my dad might have left behind that they'd be after, but she did mention the book specifically." He shrugged.

"Do they know for sure you have it?" She bit her lip, tension evident in her face.

"Not for sure, but I think they suspect. I didn't let on that I thought anything was up, and I think they don't take me seriously. Just a dumb city kid."

Cassie nodded, said nothing. Silence descended again.

"So," Grant said. "How about you tell me why that picture I was looking at spooked you so much?"

Cassie took a deep breath, visibly steeling herself. "I think I do things at night that I don't remember in the morning. I think I'm under some kind of control or something, like I'm acting out dreams or sleepwalking or who knows what. Carl always wants to stay over. He says he needs to look after me but I don't know if he's really helping or not. Some of the nights he's been there have been the worst. And when I saw that picture, it was like I was seeing one of my dreams or sleepwalks or whatever the hell they are."

"You mean you dreamed a scene like that?" Grant remembered the three men, his father on one side, the ceremonial robes and all their hands on the big knife buried in the carcass of a goat.

Cassie lowered her voice. "This going to sound nuts, but I don't know if I dreamed it. It feels too real. I think I've been there, or somewhere like it. When I saw that picture it triggered a memory and I recall, I *clearly* recall, a dream where I was lying strapped to a wooden table and men like that, dressed that way, were all around me. Except it can't be a dream, Grant. The memory is too... real. I remember how rough the table top was, how the damp the air was, the little bit of breeze their robes made when they swished. That can't be a dream. I don't know how else to explain it."

Grant pressed his lips together and kept his hands in his lap to control their trembling. After a moment, he said, "Can you remember any sounds?"

Cassie's face creased like she was about to cry. Grant reached out, took both her hands in his across the table.

"It's okay," he said. "You can trust me. We can figure this stuff out."

Cassie just nodded, face still scrunched up as tears trickled over her cheeks.

Grant took a deep breath. "There was a chant, wasn't there?" Cassie looked up sharply, so Grant carried on. "All the men and women, there were the voices of both, in a kind of repetitive, monotone chant. And over it all a deep, resounding drum, beating double hits like a giant heart."

Cassie sobbed, gripped Grant's fingers so hard he thought they might break. She stared at him with haunted eyes. "How can you know that?"

"I had the same dream."

A contemplative silence hung between them as Cassie took that in.

"What are we going to do?" she whispered.

"I don't know," he admitted. "But there's something weird going on, and we need to understand what it is."

Chapter 8

The Religious Studies department of Stuart College consisted of one very old man with wispy white hair and skin so pale it bordered on translucent. The plate on his office door named him Professor Charles McKenzie. His rheumy eyes regarded Grant with suspicion, but brightened when they saw Cassie. Grant did not miss how they roved up and down her body. Some guys never outgrew it, he supposed.

"I am sorry," the professor rasped, "but I require students to make an appointment."

"We aren't students," Cassie began. "We are hoping you can answer some questions we have about a religion we read about in an old book."

"Young lady, I might be old, but I do know how to use a telephone, and even email. Why would you drop by?" He looked like he was about to call security. Of course, if Grant or Cassie meant him ill, he'd never make it to the phone before they laid hands on him.

Grant figured that a career of outmaneuvering sneaky college students had sharpened the old man's wits to the point that trying to bullshit him would likely be futile, so he tried the truth. "We think my father might have been involved in a cult, but the name is one we've never heard before, and we can't find anything online about it. We found a couple of his books and, frankly, they're disturbing. We were in town and this is the only college for two hundred miles. We struck out at the library, but one of the ladies there suggested we speak to you."

"What is the name?"

"We didn't get her name," Grant said.

"No, young man. What is the name of the religion in which you suspect your father was involved?"

Grant and Cassie exchanged looks. He'd never said the word aloud and the thought filled him with an irrational dread.

"Kaletherex."

McKenzie looked poleaxed. He blanched, his pallid face stunned.

"Do not say that word out loud," he whispered in a harsh voice. "Wait here." He wobbled over to his desk and, with a shaky hand, scribbled something onto a slip of paper. "Here." He thrust it into Grant's hand. "This is my home address. Meet me there in two hours."

And he closed the door in their faces.

They made their way back to Grant's car in silence, both taken aback by the intensity of the man's response. Clearly, Kaletherex was more than just a name in an old book.

"That was weird," Grant said as he navigated through the narrow parking lot, careful to avoid the college kids who were either too oblivious or arrogant not to step out in front of a moving vehicle. "But he knows something. That's a good sign."

"Maybe he can tell me why I keep having those..." Cassie frowned as she glanced into the side-view mirror, then whipped around.

"What is it?"

"I thought I saw Jed and Cliff Stallard back there." She turned back around and forced a mirthless laugh. "Like those two have ever been on a college campus."

"You think they might be following us?" His anger surged and he balled one hand into a fist, barely stopping himself from punching the dashboard. He didn't know if he could handle the two of them at once, but if he laid eyes on them, he just might try.

Cassie shrugged. "Probably not. Just my imagination. Paranoid."

Grant wasn't ready to chalk it up to a flight of fancy just yet. He remembered the old saying, *Just because you're paranoid, doesn't mean they're* not *out to get you.* He turned the car around and they made two circuits of the parking lot, but saw neither the young men, nor any pickups with Scott County plates. Finally, they headed out onto the highway, Grant keeping an eye on the rear-view mirror for any signs of pursuit.

They stopped at a nearby coffee shop where they killed the next hour-and-a-half ignoring their iced mochas and talking about anything but what was truly on their minds. Cassie told him about her alcoholic father and her weird relationship with Carl, who wanted to control her, always wanted to play around, yet never pushed her for actual sex. Grant agreed that was pretty strange behavior for a young man. She told him that the only real passion Carl showed when he touched her was when it was due to the occasional bout of temper. At that, Grant shifted uncomfortably in his seat, dark thoughts in his head, but she told him to forget about it.

When she was finished, he talked about his distant relationship with his own father, and his confusion about his future. He told her how he had been in a long term relationship with Suzanne since they were both sixteen, and how she had walked out on him, dumping him via voicemail. He didn't mention how recently it had happened. Cassie was suitably appalled. They finally lapsed into a companionable silence, watching the clock as it crawled toward the appointed hour.

When it was time, they hopped back into the car and headed for McKenzie's house, which was not far from campus. They hadn't made it far when Cassie cried out. Grant hit the brakes, bringing the car to a screeching halt in the middle of the street.

"See all those police cars?" She pointed to a parking lot up ahead where a half-dozen squad cars and campus police vehicles were parked haphazardly, lights flashing. "That's the parking lot we came out of."

She was right. Grant's stomach sank as they drew closer. There was no rational reason to believe it had anything to do with him or Cassie, but he was sure it did. He pulled up alongside a cluster of students who were circled in intense conversation.

Cassie rolled down the window.

"Hey, what happened up there?"

A young man in a knit hat with a fringe down the center that make him look like a rooster walked over to the car, propped his elbows on the window, and leaned inside. Grant caught a whiff of clove cigarettes on his breath as he spoke.

"Dude, one of the professors got whacked right outside the building. Somebody beat him to death. Blood everywhere." He grinned. "Guess he gave one too many C-minuses."

"Who was it?" Grant asked, as tremors of fear

rattled through him.

"Professor McKenzie. The religious studies guy."

Cassie made a strangled noise and Grant felt the blood drain from his cheeks. "Beat him to death?" he stammered.

Clove Breath laughed. "Can you imagine? Right outside the faculty door and nobody saw a thing. How jacked-up is that? Everybody says the cops have got nothing."

Grant nodded, his mind swimming in glue as he tried to get his head around it. "Well, shit," he managed. "Poor bastard."

"Yep."

Grant pulled away from the curb, knuckles white on the wheel. His breath was fast and shallow, his heart pounded.

"I did see the Stallard boys," Cassie said in a thin, high voice. "They killed him!"

"They didn't just kill him," Grant said. "They beat him to death. In public. What the fuck are we dealing with here? Who can do something like that?" Anger battled terror in his gut. He wanted to lash out and do some beating of his own, but he wanted to run away too.

Cassie began to sob, muttering things Grant couldn't hear through the blood rushing in his ears.

"We have to go," he said, staring down the road. "We just have to get the fuck away from here. Fuck everything and everyone in Wallen's Gap!"

Cassie's breath hitched. "I can't! My family, my life, it's all there."

Grant turned on her, his eyes dark and furious. "What fucking life?" he demanded, his voice painfully loud in the confines of the car.

Cassie's anger rose to meet his. "Fuck you! It might not be much but it's all I know. You can't just run away from something like this, leave it unfinished, Grant. Don't you understand that?"

The echo of Suzanne's words stung him, fuelled his anger. "What the hell should we go back for? To get killed by the fucking Stallards ourselves?"

Cassie pointed out the back window. "That poor man was beaten to death, Grant. Because of us!"

"And what are we supposed to do about that now?" He was still shouting but Cassie's words were digging in. When she showed vigor like this it transformed her. Perhaps it was the sudden proximity of death as much as her unexpected fury, but Grant found himself battling lust along with his fear and anger.

"I don't know what we do," Cassie yelled, "but running away is not the answer!" She devolved into tears again, holding her face in her hands.

Shame rose up in Grant. "I'm sorry," he said, lowering his voice as much as possible. "The last thing we need to do is turn on each other."

Cassie nodded, saying nothing.

They drove on in heavy silence. Grant breathed deeply, one hand on Cassie's knee as she cried softly. He had no idea what to say to her. When they reached the highway he turned numbly for Wallen's Gap and stared at the road, mind still blank.

Professor McKenzie had known something, was going to share it with them. Grant hammered a punch onto the steering wheel that made Cassie jump. "Fuck! What was he going to tell us?"

"Well, he was clearly very scared and didn't want to

talk there," Cassie said quietly. "Who knows what he might have told us. But if he knew something, perhaps someone else does."

Grant caught a thought that had been skittering around the edges of his mind. "If those boys followed us up there, and followed us to McKenzie, we have to assume they're going to follow us everywhere."

Cassie twisted in her seat to look out the back. "They could be following us now!"

"I'm sure they're at least looking for us."

She took hold of his hand and squeezed so hard it hurt.

He squeezed back, a calm resolve settling over him. Professor McKenzie died because they asked him questions. He needed to honor the man's death by at least trying to get some answers. But maybe they needed to look for those answers somewhere a long way from Wallen's Gap. "Nothing is likely to happen right now," he said. "They wanted to make sure we didn't ask any more questions and I'm sure they wanted to send us a message. Scare us."

"They did a fine job of it."

Grant nodded. "So let's just keep our heads down and act like it, for now. You can go home, get your things together. I'll do the same. There's no rush if they think they're in control."

"And leaving Wallen's Gap?" Cassie asked.

"Only if and when you're ready." Grant cursed himself, but the thought persisted that he could leave any time he wanted. If Cassie wouldn't let him help her, take her away, then he could always simply leave Wallen's Gap as he had found it. He didn't really owe anyone anything, though he hated himself for thinking that. And he could try to find out more from afar, safe from the killing fists of the Stallards. But he would do his best to help Cassie first. He admired her resolve. "Don't worry. We'll deal with this."

"Really? How?" She stared at him, but he couldn't meet her eye.

Thoughts of his father's funeral, of Suzanne walking out on him, all seemed so far away. He couldn't still the subtle trembling in his chest. "I don't know yet. But we will."

Chapter 9

It was dark when they cruised back into Wallen's Gap. The events of the day had taken on a surreal quality, like they had happened to someone else. Grant steered the Camaro up the hill towards Cassie's place: a little house on a dirt road near the church.

Cassie sucked in a sharp breath as they pulled close.

"What?" Grant asked.

She nodded towards her house, where the headlights shone on two men sitting on the porch drinking cans of beer. One was Carl. The other was a rangy, stubbled man with mean eyes plainly visible even from a distance.

"Your dad?"

Cassie nodded, lips pressed into a flat line.

The men were deep in conversation and looked up as the car approached. "I could just drive on by," Grant said. "Why don't you come and stay with me tonight? No funny business," he added quickly. "Just for some peace and quiet, you know?"

"It's too late," she said, her voice dull, her expression flat. "They've seen us."

Grant cursed under his breath, pulled the car up to the curb. The men on the porch stood, beers held lazily at hip height, eyes narrowed. Grant cut the engine and made to open his door and Cassie put a hand on his thigh. Her touch thrilled him, but her intent made him cold.

"Don't," she said, voice barely above a whisper.

"I just wanted to see you to the door. You know, make sure you're okay."

"It'll only make them mad if you come with me. Look at them, they're already worked up just because we're together."

He glanced at the men, who scowled down at him. Carl shifted back and forth, as if summoning the courage to confront Grant.

"If they hurt you..."Grant began.

"It'll be just like any other day."

Grant hated the casual indifference to physical violence that was clearly a part of Cassie's make-up, but he supposed there had to be some kind of self-preservation system at work. "I can take you away, you know. Are you really that tied to this place?"

Cassie stared into his eyes for a moment, but could not hold the intensity there. "It's not that easy."

"Why not? Once I'm done here, and I nearly am, I think I'll put the cabin in the hands of a real estate agent and get the fuck out of Wallen's Gap and never look back. You could come with me."

A sharp rapping made them both jump. Cassie's dad leered in through the passenger window, Carl's wiry frame silhouetted behind him.

"Oh my God." Cassie's voice was quieter than ever as she wound down the window.

"Gonna sit out here in this piece of shit car all night?" her father asked.

Grant knew his car was certainly not a piece of shit, but wasn't about to rise to that bait.

"Grant, this is my father, Graham Brunswick.

Daddy, this is Grant Shipman."

"I know who he is and I don't appreciate him gallivanting around with my daughter."

"Sorry, Mister Brunswick," Grant said. "We were just talking."

The look Brunswick directed his way said *mind your own business*, but he spared a reply. "Talking is it? That all?"

What did that even mean? "I had to go up to Kingsville today and Cassie needed a ride."

"So you thought you'd just *give her a ride*, didya?"

"Yes, sir. Just trying to be neighborly."

"And just what the hell do you know about neighborly, city boy?"

The tension in the air thickened and Brunswick's face hardened. Grant desperately wanted to leap from the car and whip both these idiots' asses, and felt pretty sure he could do it too, but that would only be more trouble for Cassie. "I don't mean to cause any trouble," he said through gritted teeth.

"Well you done stirred up a whole mess of it. You drive off with my daughter without so much as a by your leave and you say you don't mean no trouble?"

"I don't need your permission if I want to go out," Cassie said.

Her face whipped aside as her father smacked her cheek. He had moved quicker than a striking rattlesnake. "None of your lip, girl!"

"Hey! Don't you dare hit her!" Grant shifted in his seat, opened his door.

Carl, unnoticed, had circled around behind the car and kicked Grant's door closed, banging it hard into his shoulder. It was all Grant could do to resist rubbing his shoulder, but he wasn't about to give Carl the satisfaction.

"You just get on out of here, now, and you don't so much as talk to my little girl again," Brunswick said. "Or I'll do more than hit you, boy. I got a deer rifle with your name on it and a right friendly association with the law in this town. Now get your ass on."

Cassie looked at Grant with tears in her eyes. A bead of blood glistened on her lower lip. "You have to go," she said. "It was stupid to let you drive me up here. Should have dropped me down the road or something."

"I can't leave you here."

Cassie eyes were pleading. "You have to go!" she said loudly.

Her father pulled open her door even as Carl continued to lean heavily against Grant's, trapping him.

As Cassie maneuvered herself to release the seatbelt she leaned close. "I'll sneak out and come tonight," she whispered quickly and got out of the car without another word or even catching his eye.

Grant was uncertain he had heard her correctly until she looked back as her father dragged her up towards the house and she mouthed *Tonight!* at him again. He felt a flush of relief, but it was overwhelmed by his concern, his terror, about what Brunswick and Carl might do to her in the meantime.

Carl rapped on his window. With a grimace, he wound it down about two inches.

"Don't even think about sniffing around Cassie no more," Carl slurred through the gap, his breath pungent with beer and cigarette smoke. "You get your ass on like you're told, you hear?"

Grant felt powerless. He hated the thought of leaving Cassie, but if he stayed he would only make it worse for both of them. Then again, one punch wouldn't make things that much worse, would it?

"Problem here?" a rough voice called out.

Grant looked out the back window and deflated at the sight of the Stallard boys standing on the running boards of their pickup right behind him. He hadn't even heard them pull up.

"No problem," Carl called out, with a leering grin. "Mister Shipman here was just about hightail it on out of here. Ain't that right, Shipman?"

Grinding his teeth, refusing to answer with even a nod, he started the car and pulled away. He had a tiny moment of satisfaction when Carl had to leap back to avoid having his toes run over. Grant wasn't surprised when the Stallard boys tailed him all the way back home, though they kept their distance. The last thing he saw as he turned up the dirt drive towards his cabin was their headlights, stationary in the road behind. He wondered if they were going to take up residence in his driveway all night again and what that might mean for Cassie if she did try to come to him later. He yelled a curse at the heavens and drove up to the cabin, lost and directionless. What now?

Chapter 10

The first thing Grant did upon arriving back at the cabin was retrieve the old single-shot, bolt-action .22 he'd found in the bedroom closet. He wished for something with more stopping power, but this was the only gun in the house, save the Civil War rifle. Leave it to his dad to be the only man in the southeastern United States without his own personal armory. Not that Grant was dying to shoot someone, but if the Stallards had killed the professor, they could very well kill him too.

He'd found half a box of shells in the kitchen. He slipped one into the chamber, and pocketed a handful before stepping outside. He'd been a decent shot with a rifle when he was a kid, but hadn't touched one in years. His dad had enjoyed small game hunting, mostly squirrels and rabbits, and took pride in his marksmanship with the old .22 that had belonged to Grant's grandfather. To the elder Shipman's disappointment, Grant's interest extended no farther than target shooting. It had been one of the many small differences that served to distance them from one another.

He dismissed the memory with a shake of his head and looked around for a target. He needed to test both his skill and the rifle itself. He assumed his dad had kept it clean and in good order, but what did Grant really know about rifles? Suddenly paranoid that it might, he didn't know, blow up in his face or something, he held it out away from him and fired off a shot into the soft earth up near the smokehouse.

The recoil was minimal, but he was so out of practice that, he hadn't expected it, and almost allowed the weapon to slip from his hands. He grabbed hold of it and looked around, fully expecting Carl or the Stallards to be standing somewhere nearby, pointing and laughing. Finding himself alone, he managed a laugh, reloaded the rifle, and picked out a target-- a fat pine cone about fifty yards away, limned in moonlight on the end of a long branch.

He lined up his sights, took a deep breath, relaxed, and searched for his center. Shooting was a bit like the martial arts he so enjoyed studying-- it required focus and control of your body and emotions to do it well. A familiar sense of calm confidence settled on him like a cloak and he squeezed off a measured shot.

He missed.

The bullet clipped the limb an inch to the left of his intended target. He reloaded, adjusted his aim, and grinned when the pine cone exploded in a shower of gray-brown bits. He wanted to keep shooting, but that would be a waste of time and bullets.

Emboldened by his intact skill, he decided to take a walk down the road and see if one or all of the Stallards were camped out on his drive. He wasn't sure what he'd do if he did find them there, but he wanted to at least see if they were still standing guard over him.

Using the moonlight to navigate, he kept to the forested hill above the dirt driveway. No need to provoke a confrontation unless absolutely necessary. He walked all the way to the main road and saw no one.

Why had the Stallards suddenly left him alone after following him home? It didn't make sense. It ought to be good news, but it filled him with a sense of dread. Something about the situation had changed, but what?

Movement in the trees to his left made him jump. He turned, swinging the rifle up. A group of figures drifted through the trees, glowing with a soft, spectral light. Five or six of them moved like smoke, insubstantial as they slid over the rough ground. Grant's hands shook as he gripped the weapon, his eyes wide, mouth open and dry. The group turned towards him, their hands rising, arms outstretched, reaching for him. Grant let out a strangled cry, backing up. The group moaned and wailed, speeding up as they closed the gap between themselves and Grant. He could see the trees behind them through their shimmering forms, their faces twisted in pain and longing as they shot forward, almost flying through the woods. Grant screamed and turned to run. He tripped over tangled roots and slammed into the ground, his breath escaping in a rush, the rifle tumbling from his grip.

Gasping, desperately trying to suck new air into his lungs, he rolled over, hands raised against what ghostly assault might be coming, but nothing was there. The forest was still and dark.

Shaking, nauseated with shock, he got to his feet and retrieved the weapon. Just how many strange and frightening things could happen in this godforsaken shithole of a town? He wanted to get back into his car and keep driving until Wallen's Gap was a distant memory, but all he could see in his mind's eye was Cassie, looking back and mouthing *Tonight!* He couldn't leave her now. What he really needed was answers. Understanding was the only defence against whatever was going on here.

He headed back up towards the cabin and thoughts of the strange book in the smokehouse drifted through his mind. If he wanted to know more about what was going on, perhaps some answer could be found there. He needed something to go on. He grabbed a flashlight from the cabin and trudged up hill.

He found one answer when he reached the smokehouse, but it was to the question of why the Stallards had stopped camping in his driveway, not what he might do for Cassie. The door was kicked in and the compartment where the book had been now stood open. He could see scrapes and indentations where it had been pried open with a crowbar. The Stallards had taken it. It was too great a coincidence to have been anyone else. Their mother had tried to get it, they'd shown up poking around. It had to be them.

"Son of a bitch!"

Knowing it was futile, he reached inside and felt around inside the hollowed-out space. No book.

And then his fingers fell on something small and hard. It had a waxy feel to it, a short narrow thing, with lumps and a slightly sharp, flat end.

He drew it out carefully and held it up in the beam of the flashlight. With a bark of surprise and disgust, he dropped it on the dirt floor. A finger. Stunned, thinking he must have got that wrong, he crouched for another look. Sure enough, it was a finger, but ancient and blackened, like something from *The Mummy*. The nail was long and ragged, that must have been the sharp end he felt. The skin was tight across the knuckle bones, and the end that should be attached to a hand was dry and hard, the skin edges flaky around the circle of bone sticking out. A smooth edge on the bone, like the finger had been cut off with a sharp knife. *Before or after death?* he wondered.

It was small, no surprise the Stallards had missed it. And if his dad thought it important enough to hide along with the book, it must have some value. He picked it up again, held it up in the flashlight beam again for a closer look. A sensation drifted through him, like the feeling when a spider runs over your arm. A kind of repulsion that shivers deep in the core. But something else too. A sense almost of power, of direction. Like there was something about the dessicated old finger that reached beyond the obvious and into realms less traveled.

"Where did my dad get you?" Grant said softly to himself. "And why did he keep you?"

The finger flexed at the middle knuckle and twisted, pointed out the door of the smokehouse.

Grant cried out in alarm and the finger hit the dirt again. Panting, heart jackhammering his ribs, he stared at the thing on the floor. A part of him was embarrassed that he had screamed like a little girl. Another part told him to run the hell away and keep going until Wallen's Gap was far in his rear view mirror.

The finger was still and straight on the ground, inert. He crouched and prodded it. Nothing. Surely, he'd imagined it. But somehow, he knew that wasn't the case.

With a trembling hand, he picked it up and held it by the stump of bone. It was hard, dry and immobile again. He felt an urge to ask another question, felt the insane certainty that, in some way, it would answer. The sensation of power swelled inside him. And with it, the revulsion, a blackness soaking into the edges of his soul. This thing was clearly potent, yet it was undoubtedly dangerous too.

Grant tucked it into his shirt pocket, unsure quite why, but reluctant to leave it behind. He grabbed the rifle, and stalked out into the night.

Right now, his most fervent wish was that the Stallards would return. In the mood he was in, he figured he could take all three of them at once.

"Dammit to fucking hell."

Chapter 11

Grant sat up late into the night, watched the hands of the clock creep past eleven, through midnight, towards one a.m. Cassie had said she would come later, and there were no Stallards camping in the driveway to stop her this time. Or were there?

Exhausted, but too wired to even contemplate sleep, he took the .22 and headed out again. He left the flashlight behind and relied on moonlight to show the way. If anyone was waiting down the drive, no sense in alerting them to his presence. He crept through the trees, all the way to the road and sure enough, the Stallards were nowhere to be seen. So perhaps Cassie was not coming to him after all. He ground his teeth, wondering if she had changed her mind and decided not to come, or if, for some reason, she couldn't come. He remembered the slap through the car window, the anger and hatred plain on Brunswick's face. And Carl's. He imagined Cassie bruised and beaten, locked in her bedroom.

He felt helpless and it only made him more furious. What could he do? He wanted to protect her, but she went willingly with her father. Of course, he couldn't blame her for that. He was her father and she had to make her own decisions. But Grant was falling for her, ached deep in his bones to protect her, and he knew the only way he could really protect her was to take her away from Wallen's Gap. He needed to convince her there really wasn't anything to hold her there. These were big decisions, but Cassie was abused and scared and the only way out was all the way out. That didn't even begin to take into account what else might be happening in her life. The stories about sleepwalking and finding blood on herself, her dreams that matched his vision in that hideous book. Not to mention all the other weird shit that he desperately tried to ignore.

Standing in the deep shadow of a pine, Grant jumped as something squirmed against his chest. The finger was still in his shirt pocket, almost forgotten. Reluctant to reach in, he pulled his pocket forward and leaned out into the moonlight to see. The finger sat in the lint at the bottom of his pocket half curled like a comma. As he looked, it straightened and curled up, straightened and curled up, jabbing at his shirt.

"Shit!" He sprang backward, the severed digit tumbling out onto the dirt. He'd almost managed to convince himself the scene in the smokehouse had been his imagination. Clearly not. As he watched, the digit once again flexed and extended, somehow conveying insistence in its motion.

"Are you pointing me to something?"

The finger fell still. As Grant drew a breath, it flexed again, more insistent than ever. With a small intake of breath, he picked it up and held it by the smooth stub of bone. The thing squirmed in his grip. He turned his body and the finger crooked forward, jabbing at the air. He turned further and the digit twisted and squirmed. When he turned back, it jabbed again, pointed up over the hill in the direction of higher ground, somewhere north of Wallen's Gap.

"There's nothing up there but more freaking trees," Grant said softly. "What are you trying to tell me?"

The finger stiffened and all sensation of animation left it. Grant held a hard, dead bone wrapped in age-blackened skin once more.

"Am I really talking to a dead man's fucking finger?" he said, and dropped it back into his pocket. Once more the sensation of dread and power washed through him, enhanced him somehow. There was no doubt this ancient bodypart had been alive and moving moments ago, even if it was dead again now. He didn't like anything about it, considered throwing it away into the night-shrouded forest.

Immediately despair swept over him. He could never throw this thing away, he needed it! He took a shuddering breath, the desperation of the feeling made his guts icy. "Dad kept it for a reason," he said aloud to the night, rationalizing his reasons for holding onto it. At least for the time being. He stomped back up to the cabin, locked the doors and fell into a rough, restless sleep filled with monsters and threats he could not quite recall upon waking.

The morning dawned clear and cool. Grant dragged himself from bed not long after sun up, still dog tired but beyond trying to sleep any more. He felt like he hadn't slept properly since he got to this shithole town. During his tossing and turning he'd come to one conclusion. First thing today he would go to Cassie's house and insist that he talk to her. If he had to beat his way to her through Brunswick and Carl, or any other fucker, so be it. He was at the end of his patience.

Grant downed coffee and toast to quell the hollow rumble in his gut, and drove into town. As he cruised along the main street, it occurred to him that it was still only a little after seven and that was too early to go calling on anyone. He should at least try to start without pissing them all off. The diner was just opening, so Grant pulled up and went inside for more coffee.

As he sat and sipped, he stared into a large mirror on the wall opposite the counter. A crack ran down the wall behind the man, the plaster separating as the line of darkness widened. Grant froze, eyes wide. The crack opened further and flames appeared to flicker inside. Dark fingers with black talons slipped through and gripped the ragged edge, taking hold of the other side, as though they could rip the wall apart so whatever it was could step through. The owner turned from his grill and made to walk right past the yawning fracture.

Grant spun in his seat. "No, look out!"

The diner owner scowled. "Something wrong with you, boy?"

The wall behind him was smooth and unblemished, apart from grease stains on the pale paint. "No, sorry," Grant said weakly. "It's nothing."

The man shook his head, disgust evident in his expression. His eyes seemed to glow momentarily red as he turned away.

Suppressing a shudder, Grant returned to his coffee. The sooner he got to Cassie and out of Wallen's Gap, the better.

As the clock on the wall ticked past eight o'clock, he went back to his car and drove up to the Brunswick house.

The street was quiet, no people walking and only one or two other vehicles sliding slowly by. He parked along the curb and walked to the front door. Before he lost his nerve, he knocked firmly. Footsteps rang out almost immediately and the door flew open.

Brunswick stood there wearing nothing but striped boxers and filthy, stained white t-shirt. "What the hell do you want, city boy? Didn't I tell you to stay away?"

Grant stood tall, refused to be intimidated. "I want to talk to Cassie."

"What did you say to me?"

"I want to talk to Cassie."

"Yeah? Well, she don't wanna talk to you. You just run on, now, before I get my shotgun and encourage you along."

Brunswick began to close the door and Grant put a hand against it. He looked past Brunswick and yelled out, "Cassie! It's Grant. You there?"

Brunswick yanked the door wide open and slapped a palm into Grant's chest, and shoved him back across the porch. "Who the hell do you think you are, boy? Get outta here!"

Grant snarled, grabbed Brunswick's wrist and twisted it away from his chest. Brunswick yelped and half-turned, fell to one knee so his bones wouldn't snap.

"Cassie!" Grant shouted again. "I need to talk to you!"

"She ain't here." Carl stepped out of the shadow of the hallway onto the porch.

Releasing Brunswick, Grant turned to face the skinny stoner.

Brunswick stood, rubbed at his wrist, as he grinned.

"Ain't here," he echoed.

"Where is she?" Grant asked.

Carl laughed, shook his head, and muttered something under his breath. Grant didn't catch the words, but the tone was amused.

"She's gone to stay with her aunt in Kingsville for a few weeks." Brunswick grinned. "Said you was getting on her nerves, kind of stalker-like."

"Bullshit. I dropped her off here last night. You know that. How could she have gone back to Kingsville?"

"I don't know, a car?" Carl, still chuckling, gestured into the house. "You wanna go inside and have a look around, smart guy?"

Brunswick glared at Carl, then his face softened as he cottoned on. "Yeah, that's right. Go on in, have a look around."

Grant stared at them hard, trying to measure their intent. Were they hoping to lure him in so they could jump him out of the sight of witnesses? Then again, there wasn't anyone around to witness the act, and he doubted anyone in town would lift a finger to help or even call the police. Fuck it, he didn't care if that was their plan, he had no fear of these two stringy losers. Bracing for a brawl, heart pounding and all his senses alive, he strode into the house and started searching room by room. Carl and Brunswick stood in the hall, laughing at him. It didn't take long to search the whole place, small as it was, calling Cassie's name as he went.

He lingered when he got to her bedroom. It certainly looked like she'd packed up and left. The closet stood open, bare hangers dangling skeleton-like in the glow of the cheap lamp on the bedside table. The dresser drawers were similarly empty. There were no personal effects, no pictures on the wall, nothing. Only a door hanger spelling out "Cassie" in spangled script bore testimony to the room's former inhabitant. If she'd been abducted, they wouldn't have stopped to let her pack, would they?

He dismissed the doubts with a shake of his head. "Tell me where she is," he demanded again.

"At her aunt's," Brunswick said.

"In Richmond," Carl said.

"Kingsville," Brunswick corrected. He put his hand on the stoner's shoulder. "Carl, step outside for a minute, would you?"

Carl sniggered. "Oh yeah, Kingsville. Knew it was something like that." He shot an unreadable glance at Grant. "Holler if you need me."

Brunswick turned to face Grant. "Now, you listen good. I don't like you, and I don't owe you the truth, but here it is anyhow. Cassie couldn't decide between you and Carl and she felt like you was both putting too much pressure on her. She left, and I ain't telling you where she is."

"Bullshit." Grant felt his anger boiling. "Where the hell is she?"

Brunswick was suddenly serious, his face hard. "She ain't anywhere for you to find, boy. Now, I ain't gonna tell you again. Get outta here."

A rough voice came from behind. "Problem here?"

Grant's blood ran cold. Jesse Stallard stood in the doorway. Beyond, through the open front door, Grant saw the other two Stallard boys lounging in their truck, parked at the curb.

He grimaced. Five on one odds were not good, especially with all three Stallards. They were a much greater threat than either Carl or Brunswick. Besides, as much as he wanted to bust some skulls, what he really wanted was to find Cassie.

He stiffened, looked from Stallard to Brunswick, and shook his head. "No. I was just leaving." Summoning as much dignity as he could muster under the circumstances, he strode directly at Stallard, who held his ground for only a split-second before giving way. Grant shouldered him aside, rather than brushing past him, but Stallard only chuckled. "City pussy."

Something inside Grant snapped. "What the fuck did you say?"

Jesse grinned. "I called you a pussy, pussy."

Grant growled and rushed the tall Stallard, his fist striking out with all his pent up frustrations and fear. The impact across the redneck's cheek was a rush of satisfaction and Jesse cried out, stumbling drunkenly to one side, eyes wide in surprise. Grant followed him and delivered two more heavy punches and Jesse dropped unconscious to the floor. Cliff and Jed came racing across the lawn as Carl ran from the house, yelling incoherently.

Grant turned on Carl, landing one good shot on the rangy stoner's chin before he was pummelled from both sides by the remaining Stallard brothers. He roared and spat, struck out left and right, letting all his anger go, beyond caring any more. He felt the impacts from all sides, but refused to go down, stumbling back and forth as he grit his teeth and fought back. No way was he going down without giving them something to remember him by.

"Enough!" The voice was a whip crack in the early morning air.

Grant was stunned when the fight stopped almost instantly. He swung a couple more shots even as all the boys moved away.

"Pastor Edwin," Graham Brunswick said. "Ain't nothing to worry about here."

"That right?" Edwin said. "Get along, boys."

Jesse Stallard moaned, coming around as his brothers picked him up, held him between them. They nodded at their father, grinning, more amused than chastised.

"This ain't the time or the place," Edwin went on. "Now all o'ya get along out of here."

The Stallard brothers returned to their truck and Carl and Graham strode into the house and closed the door, leaving Grant alone on the front grass with the pastor. Grant panted for breath, his knuckles cut and throbbing, his face and body pulsing with pain. The pastor stared at him for a moment, his expression blank, then returned to his own house next door.

Grant stood alone, confused. What the fuck was that all about? The rush of punching out a Stallard was lost again in the fear and confusion of Wallen's Gap. Grant limped back to his car. He needed to find Cassie. Nothing else mattered.

Chapter 12

Grant rolled into town, his mood as black as the clouds that hung low on the horizon. He knew Cassie hadn't taken off on her own, but the slightest doubt remained. What if she really had left? He couldn't entirely blame her if she had. Her life sucked. But he was sure he'd felt a connection between them, and she had indicated she was tired of Carl. Then again, she'd also indicated that she couldn't seem to shake the guy.

"What am I doing?" he said aloud. "Pull yourself together, Grant." He steered the car into a parking space on the main drag and sat for a moment, gathering his thoughts.

He wanted two things: answers about Kaletherex, and to find Cassie. If Cassie had left of her own accord, there probably wasn't much he could do about it. If she hadn't, he was convinced the key to finding her lay with whatever secret hid behind the sinister name. Maybe he was stuck in Wallen's Gap for a while longer after all. After a few minutes' contemplation, he decided to give the library another go.

Since he already had a library card, he was able to avoid another annoying question-and-answer session with the aged librarian, and got right to work. Settling in at one of the computer stations, he decided to take a different tack. McKenzie had known something about Kaletherex, so he decided to start by researching the recently-deceased professor.

The first several results were accounts of the unsolved murder, sudden big news in the area, but at the bottom of the page he found a link to the professor's page on the college website. He skimmed the brief bio and list of publishing credits, and one title leaped out at him. *Ancient Mysticism in Appalachia.* That sounded promising.

A quick web search revealed the book was out of print and unavailable in electronic form, but when he checked the library catalog, he was surprised to find it listed. His sudden euphoria turned quickly to disappointment when he saw that the book was checked out. He muttered a curse, drawing the attention of the librarian, who frowned and raised a finger to her lips. Since she and Grant were the only people in the place, shushing him was a bit absurd, but he didn't want to get on her bad side just now. He nodded and adopted a duly chastened expression.

He made a few more fruitless web searches and then, on a whim, checked to see if Cassie had a Facebook page. No luck. He sighed. The book was his only possible lead. Time to go for it.

He approached the front desk and waited politely while the librarian pretended not to notice him. She puttered about, shifting items around and opening drawers to inspect their contents. She was clearly doing no actual work. Finally, she let out a deep sigh and looked up.

"I was interested in a particular book," Grant said, forcing a smile, "but it's checked out. Any chance you could tell me when it's due to be returned?" He handed her a slip of paper with the title and author.

Pursing her lips, she turned the paper over and examined the back for some inexplicable reason. She stared at Grant for five uncomfortable heartbeats before nodding and turning to her computer.

"It is long overdue," she said after a few mouse clicks. "Let me see. Oh." Her wrinkled faced reddened. "I'm afraid I can't help you."

Grant couldn't believe his shitty luck. "Can you at least tell me who was the last person to check it out?"

The woman looked him in the eye, seeming to really see him for the first time.

"Andrew Shipman."

Grant wandered out of the library in a half-daze. Here was a solid connection. There had to be something in McKenzie's book that could help him understand what the hell his father had been into. Now, if he could only find the book. Surely it was somewhere in all the boxes he'd packed up.

He was so deep in thought that he almost walked right into the girl leaning against his car. He looked up in surprise as she greeted him.

"Hey there. You're the new guy." She had wavy, brown hair, big hazel eyes, and straight, white teeth-- a rarity in Wallen's Gap. She wore hip-huggers and a tight tee shirt that emphasized her curves. She cocked her hip and he caught a glimpse of flat, tanned abs and a pink thong.

"I know I am." He wished he had come up with a smarter retort, but his reply must have tickled her funny bone. She giggled and touched his forearm with the tip of a heavily lacquered fingernail.

"You're cute. I'm Jazy."

"Grant." He racked his brain for a way to extricate himself from the conversation. The girl was smoking hot, and not just by Wallen's Gap standards, but he wanted to find the book, and maybe find Cassie.

"I been wanting to catch you since I saw you drive by in this sweet car a couple days ago," Jazy said. "When I saw it just now, I finally plucked up the courage to stop and say hello. You can probably imagine how dull it gets around here, when you know everyone and there's nothing new and exciting going on."

"Sure, I guess."

"Are you okay?" Jazy took a step closer and looked up at him in genuine concern.

"Yeah, sorry, just got a lot on my mind."

"I know."

"You do?" How could she possibly know what was going on?

"I lost my daddy too, not so long ago." Sadness dulled her eyes, but she forced a smile. "You just gotta give it time. Nothing else helps."

Grant felt a lump forming in his throat. It wasn't out of sadness over the loss of his dad, but for this bit of simple kindness and concern. He'd experienced precious little of such normal human interactions since arriving in Wallen's Gap. He cleared his throat.

"Thanks." Then a thought occurred to him. "Say, do you know Cassie Brunswick?"

"Why sure." Jazy smiled. "Of course, everybody knows everybody around here, but me and Cassie are friends. She's sweet."

"You wouldn't know where I could find her, would you?" If Jazy and Cassie were friends, maybe the girl knew something.

Jazy brought her fingers to her lips and stared at him, her eyes gleaming with sympathy. "Oh my God, I didn't even think. Of course it was you."

"What was me?" A cold, heavy weight sagged inside of him.

"She called me late last night, all upset because she thinks she still loves Carl but she also likes some new fellow, and the pressure's getting to her. And apparently all kinds of other things are going on. She wouldn't tell me who the other guy was, and I figured it was a local boy." She made a face. "Anyhow, she said she was going to go stay with her cousin or some such, she just couldn't handle staying in town until her head was straight. She was calling me for advice, and I told her sure, she should go and give herself time and space to think. Oh, don't look like that." She put her hands on his shoulders and pulled him close. He was keenly aware of her breasts pressing against his chest. "I'm sure she won't be gone too long, and I don't think she'll pick that Carl."

Grant stared over her head at the mountains, their peaks hidden by low-hanging rain clouds. So Cassie really had left on her own. It was hard to believe, but there it was in unrequested corroboration. First Suzanne, then Cassie. Whatever. If she actually found it difficult to choose between him and that Carl dipshit, he didn't need her in his life. He would never understand women. At least she was well away from the genetic traffic circle that was Wallen's Gap, and that was the main thing, right? With any luck she would stay away from her mean father and that idiot Carl. .

"Come on. I know just the thing to cheer you up." Jazy took him by the hand and led him down the street. He wondered what she had in mind as she took him down a side street. The asphalt gave way to a rutted dirt and gravel road, and weeds grew tall in the cracks in the sidewalk.

They arrived at a small diner, the name painted on the dirty window proclaiming it *The Lyons' Den*. As she pushed the door open, the sounds of music and cheerful conversation poured out. He raised an eyebrow at Jazy. This was about as unlike Wallen's Gap as you could get. She grinned and pushed him in ahead of her.

The diner was dim and filled with the aroma of greasy Southern cooking. The few patrons, every one of them African-American, only spared the new arrivals a passing glance before smiling or nodding at Jazy and returning to their conversations. John Lee Hooker belted out a mournful blues tune from an old-school jukebox in the corner. The atmosphere wrapped around Grant like a comfortable old blanket.

"You feel better already, don't you?" Jazy still held his hand, and he realized he didn't mind so much. "Welcome to the only place in Wallen's Gap where people actually mean it when they're nice to each other."

She introduced him to Amos Lyons, the proprietor, an elderly man with hair as white as his skin was dark. His teeth and eyes were matching shades of very pale yellow, but his smile was friendly. He shook Grant's hand, warned him to "Watch out for Miss Jazy, she's trouble!" in a stage whisper, and handed them each a bottle of Mountain Dew.

"I'm not a big Mountain Dew guy," he said as they

sat down at a table near the jukebox.

"Take a drink." Jazy smiled as he took a gulp and surprise registered on his face. "It's really Budweiser. I ain't twenty-one yet. Of course, he charges six dollars a bottle, but every once in a while it's worth it to sit back, listen to some music, and have a cold one. Don't you think?"

"Definitely. No offense, but this town is depressing as hell." He took a long pull of beer, enjoying the flavor as the ice cold brew slaked his thirst.

"You don't have to tell me. God, I want to get out of here so bad, but I don't know how." She shrugged and let her head hang.

"Hey, don't do that." Grant put a finger under her chin and tipped her face up. "You're the only ray of sunshine around here. Don't let this place beat you."

"I'm not college material and I don't know anything else to do with myself. I thought about dancing, you know." She pantomimed a pole dance with such a goofy look on her face that Grant had to laugh. "But that ain't me."

"There's always a way. You just have to hang in there until you figure out what it is." Grant's thoughts turned to Cassie. Was there a way out for her? Did she even want one, or was she going to come back and choose Carl? He kicked himself. Stupid. Cassie had made her choice, and a part of him was happy for her. She was smart enough to get away from everything, for a little while at least, even if that meant getting away from him too. So be it. He turned his attention back to Jazy.

By the time they'd downed a few beers, a half a rack of ribs, and the crunchiest, greasiest onion rings he'd ever eaten, he had managed to put Cassie out of his mind. Jazy wanted to know everything about him, his life, and the problems with his father. She laughed at all the right places and kept touching his arm in a familiar way. She adored the idea that he was a musician and made him promise to play for her soon. When her hand crept down to his lap, he knew it was time to leave. He left enough cash on the table to cover their check plus a generous tip, and followed her out the door, his eyes only drifting from her hips long enough to see two young men grin and give him the thumbs-up.

He smiled as he closed the door. Maybe things were finally looking up for him.

Chapter 13

"This is it." Grant ushered Jazy inside the cabin, closed the door behind them, and locked it, vowing that any Stallard who interrupted them would pay in blood.

"Not bad," she said, looking around. "I've never been up to this part of the mountain. It's nice and quiet here away from town." She turned and draped her arms around his neck. "Very romantic."

He drew her close and pressed his lips to hers. They fell onto the old couch, arms and legs entwined. He ran his hands up and down her body, half his mind refusing to give up thoughts of Cassie and the other half marveling at Jazy's fine curves. That second half quickly won out and he pulled the t-shirt off over her head. Passion lent them urgency and it was no time before they were both naked and thoughts of any kind beyond the carnal found no further purchase in Grant's beer-buzzed brain. He forced himself to take his time, let all his frustrations and concerns boil away in an unquenched furnace of desire.

By the end they had migrated to the rug in front of the big fireplace. Grant wanted to get up and light it, but their bodies were still hot and glistened with a fine sheen of sweat, and he was reluctant to remove Jazy's head from his chest, or her leg from where it lay hooked over his. She ran a finger in gentle swirls over his belly, sending pleasant shivers through his body.

"You wanna take me away for a few days?" she asked dreamily.

Grant frowned. That seemed like a strange and sudden request. "Take you away?"

"Sure. You know, go somewhere fun and exciting. I know I have to work my own way out of this shitty town, but maybe you and I could take a few days, you know? We can have some more fun like this, and maybe I'll get some ideas for my escape plan." She brushed his earlobe with her soft lips, making him shudder with pleasure.

He tried to ignore the urge that was already stirring again inside of him, and focused on the moment and her request. He wanted to say something along the lines of *I hardly know you, why would we go away together?* but given what they had just done, that seemed like the wrong way to go. "I dunno, I have a still lot to sort out here," he said. "Maybe we could, you know, just hang out around here, and maybe go away in a week or so once I've got everything straightened out?"

She pushed herself up onto one elbow, and stretched, displaying her figure to full effect. Her hazel eyes, suddenly flinty, gazed at him through a curtain of tousled hair. "I got me the wanderlust." She whispered the last word like an incantation. "I want to be spontaneous. Let's go right now! The cabin will still be here when we get back."

He reluctantly tore his gaze away from her amazing breasts. "Right now?"

"Yeah! Let's get in that hot car of yours and just go somewhere. It don't have to be anywhere fancy. I just want to go."

Grant laughed to cover a sudden unease. Guilty thoughts of Cassie flitted through his mind and Jazy's strange insistence on going away raised uncomfortable suspicions. From the corner of his eye he saw his shirt draped over the arm of the sofa and the material of the top pocket shifted and bucked. He winced and pulled Jazy in for a kiss before she could notice. As they moved apart again, he rolled her over to his other side to put her back to the hideous dismembered finger and brushed back her hair. "I'm too beat to drive anywhere right now," he said. "Why don't we talk about it again in the morning?"

She pouted, but nodded. "Sure. But what are you gonna do to keep me entertained till morning?" She sat up, straddled his hips and put her palms on his chest. She shifted back and forth, eyes alive with a mischievous gleam.

Grant refused to give a moment's notice to the thoughts tumbling over each other in his mind and reached up for her again.

The dawn pushed shadows from the bedroom. They had retreated to the comforts of the bed at some very late hour of the night. Or early morning depending how one measured such things. Grant watched Jazy sleeping, half-covered by the sheets. She was one gorgeous girl, but the cold and sober light of day brought with it troubling concerns.

He slipped from the bed, careful not to rouse her, and tiptoed out into the front room. He began searching through boxes and it wasn't long before he pulled out a small paperback volume. *Ancient Mysticism in Appalachia* by Professor Charles McKenzie. His mind buzzed as he imagined his father checking the book out of the library. He thought of the horrible leatherbound volume the Stallards had stolen. The blackened finger they had missed. Coupled with this book, his own concerns and Cassie's nightmares, not to mention McKenzie's violent death, everything about Wallen's Gap took on a darker hue. And something else, something that had been bothering the edges of his conscious mind for a while that he couldn't ignore. His father's death. He remembered what the waitress in the diner had said just a few days ago, even though it seemed like a lifetime. *So young for a heart attack.*

There was no family history of heart disease that Grant knew of and his father had never been a smoker, or a particularly heavy drinker. By the time Grant had arrived in Wallen's Gap, the local doctor had already made the official announcements and the memorial service was for a man already cremated. Grant's hands began to tremble. His father had definitely been a part of this Kaletherex group, but had he perhaps found things he didn't like? Had he learned things he shouldn't have? Had he perhaps not died of a heart attack at all?

Grant shook his head, rubbed one hand back over his hair. This town had him so confused, so many things made no sense. Or seemed to be far more complicated than they needed to be. Was he losing his mind? His thoughts fell to Cassie again and a burning guilt rose up from his gut. He had been so ready to believe Jazy the day before, but now even that seemed unreal. Was checking the book out of the library one of the last things his father had done?

He opened it up and began looking through the table of contents. There were chapters on all kinds of Appalachian myths and legends, but towards the end of the book was a chapter entitled, *Cults and Secret Societies of Appalachia.* Grant swallowed, nerves cooling his spine. He turned to the chapter and began scanning the sub-headings. He got to one that made him gasp, *The Banishing of Kaletherex.*

"You okay, sweetie?"

Grant jumped, dropped the book in his lap. Jazy stood in the doorway, leaning against the frame wearing nothing but one of his t-shirts. With the morning light behind her, she was hotter than ever. "Yeah, fine," he said, hoping she didn't notice the tremor in his voice.

"What's that you're reading?"

"Oh, just going through some of dad's stuff, you know. Trying to decide what to keep, what to throw away or give to charity."

"Uh-huh." She rang her tongue slowly over her lips. "So, what about that idea of you and me going away for a few days?"

The nerves and unspent energy that were making Grant twitchy didn't dissipate. "You seem pretty anxious to go away right now."

A flash of annoyance darkened her eyes for a moment, then it was gone. She smiled and peeled the t-shirt off, stood before him unashamedly, and amazingly, naked. "We can put the trip off for an hour or two if you want *breakfast,*" she said.

Grant stared at her for a long time, trying to ignore his body's insistent and obvious desires. He tore his eyes away. "I can't, not right now."

Her voice was suddenly hard, angry. "Are you

serious?"

He refused to look up at her again, but stood and gathered his discarded clothes from the night before, began pulling them on. "I'm really sorry, Jazy, I'd love to take off with you, but I just have to... You know, I have to..." This was wrong. Everything here was all wrong.

"Have to what?" Her tone was cold.

"I have so much stuff to do with my dad's things." He stuffed the paperback book into the back pocket of his jeans, dragged on his shirt. The finger in the top pocket twitched and writhed momentarily.

Jazy stalked past him, collected her own clothes from the floor. As she dressed she said, "I can't believe you're turning me down." Something in her eyes scared him. A deep, abiding hatred seemed to have sprung up from nowhere and burned into him relentlessly.

He felt the need to reassure her, if only to not make any more of an enemy here. "I'm not turning you down, Jazy, really. I just have so many things on my mind. Let me get some stuff sorted out today and we can come back here later and..."

"Take me back to town, Grant."

He reached for her. "Come on, Jazy, don't be..."

She slapped his hand away. "Take me back to town."

A glacier had descended between them and Grant knew it was pointless to try to do anything about it. "Okay."

They drove back down to Wallen's Gap in icy silence. The book pressed uncomfortably into Grant's backside, but he didn't want to move it anywhere that Jazy might see it. The finger in his pocket jerked and twitched occasionally. When they reached the main street, he drove slowly, wondering what to do, what to say. He pulled up at a T-junction and Jazy opened the door and got out.

"Hey!" he called after her, stunned. "Hey, Jazy, come on."

She walked away without a word or a backward glance.

Chapter 14

Grant walked into the *Cup Of Joe* diner, feeling thoroughly bemused. He needed coffee and time to think. What exactly had happened this morning? His suspicions grew on each other like mold on old bread, hideous and consuming. More than ever he wanted to get into his car and drive away, far from Wallen's Gap, and never look back. But it seemed that Jazy had been determined to make him do just that and he couldn't help wondering why. Her mood, her disposition toward him, had changed so quickly and so dramatically. Over his confusion, his guilt sat heavier than anything else. He couldn't get thoughts of Cassie from his mind and felt as though he'd let her down. But he didn't know what to do. The finger in his shirt pocket writhed almost constantly and he couldn't bring himself to look at that either. It felt as much a danger as it might be a help, and how the hell could a disembodied finger keep moving around anyway? For some reason, though, it was important to keep it with him, though he had no idea why. Surely he was losing his mind, hallucinating, imagining conspiracies everywhere.

On the counter were various candies for sale. One was a tin of small, round breath mints. He forced a smile to man behind the counter as he bought a tin, even though the man looked at him like he was a giant walking turd that was smearing up the diner by its presence alone. Grant went directly from the counter into the bathroom and tipped the contents of the small tin into the garbage bin. He took the finger from his shirt pocket, refusing to even look at it, and pushed it into the tin, which he jammed deep into the hip pocket of his jeans. He wanted to throw the hideous thing away, but something compelled him to keep it. Even though it darkened the edges of his mind, laid a stain on his very soul, he couldn't get rid of it, couldn't even leave it behind somewhere. He had to keep it with him, even if he had no explanation why. At least now he wouldn't constantly feel its horrible movements.

He pulled the book from his back pocket, thumbed through to the chapter on the banishing of Kaletherex. He read the first few paragraphs, standing in the coolness of the bathroom. It talked of a man who had moved to Wallen's Gap when it was little more than a camp, and how that man had uncovered the activity of a very nasty group of people praising a thing called Kaletherex. A *daemon* the book said. Grant paused, shook his head. A demon?

He read on.

The man who arrived in Wallen's Gap was appalled at the things this group did in the name of the daemon Kaletherex. He vowed to put an end to their deviant ministry, even if it killed him. This chapter is the best account of this legend I could put together, collected from various members of the Wallen's Gap community, though I should point out that getting any information at all was not easy. The people of this remote mountain town are distrustful of outsiders and reluctant to share any knowledge of this old myth. Most claim to have never even heard of it. But a few bits and pieces of information began to surface and I was able to put together this account, of how that weary traveler took on and supposedly banished the demon Kaletherex. That man's name was Josiah Brunswick and this, to the best of my ability, is his story.

Grant stopped reading the old professor's words, his blood turning to icicles in his veins. Josiah Brunswick? Like Cassie Brunswick? Was it even vaguely possible they were related? In a town like this, it was highly unlikely that two unrelated families would shard the same surname. He needed to learn more about this and quickly. He stuffed the book back into his pocket and headed out into the diner. He needed a big coffee while he sat and read the rest of the account.

He pushed open the bathroom door and stepped out, and something hard struck him across the cheek. With a cry of pain and surprise, he fell to one knee, his vision blurred.

"You just can't take any kind of hint, can ya?" Jesse Stallard said, and kicked him in the ribs.

Pain blossoming through his chest Grant hurled himself at Jesse, and caught him on the chin with a hard right cross. Jesse staggered back and Grant bore him to the ground. But, before he could do any damage, Jed and Cliff were on top of him. He struggled to break loose as they hauled him to his feet, but the two were strong, and held his arms in twin vise grips. Jesse kicked him in the groin and Grant's knees gave way. Next he knew, the three brothers set to punching and kicking him as he curled up in a ball and tried to shield himself from the worst of the blows. He caught sight of the diner's owner standing by the front door, one hand on the lock as he watched the street outside.

"Help me!" Grant croaked, but the man didn't even turn to look.

The blows became distant and the pain a dull roar all over his body as consciousness receded. In a dark haze, he was dimly aware of being lifted, and felt the cold air of outside wash over him before the hard, rutted metal floor of a pick-up truck rose to meet him with a jarring impact.

Everything hurt. He swam in and out of awareness as the truck roared to life and pulled away. There was nothing else in the back with him and he slid left and right as they drove, banging into the metal sides with dull thumps and grunts of pain. Was he going to die now? Thoughts of throwing himself from the truck, heedless of further injury, rose in his mind. Anything was better than lying here awaiting his fate.

He braced himself to rise despite the pain in every part of him, pushed himself to hands and knees. Something hit him in the jaw and he fell sideways, stunned again. Through a haze of pain and semi-consciousness he saw Cliff Stallard sitting on the side of the pick-up, hanging onto the roof-mounted hunting lights with one hand, leering down at him. Cliff raised his boot again and Grant gave up and let the darkness in. His last thought was that he had let Cassie down and would never get the chance to save her, to help her away from Wallen's Gap.

Chapter 15

Cassie looked down at Grant with an expression of deepest regret. She reached down to touch his battered face, and he flinched away. She frowned and her expression grew dark.

And then her hair darkened. And her eyes.

It was Jazy looking down on him.

"I told you we should go away together. Now look what's happened to you."

He tried to answer but could only manage a dull moan. He hurt all over.

"Aw, does it hurt?" Her words were sympathetic, but cold pleasure gleamed in her eyes. "Here, I'll kiss you where it hurts."

She leaned in close, and her face... rippled. Her hair fell out and her skin turned gray and scaly. Her teeth sharpened into yellow fangs, and her face elongated into a snout.

Grant thrashed about as the thing that had been Jazy drew closer. He wanted to fight it off, but his arms were like lead.

"What's wrong?" the creature hissed. "Don't you think I'm pretty?"

He watched in horror as it flicked out its tongue and licked him across the forehead.

"No!" He screamed and sat up.

"Settle yourself down, son. You ain't in no condition

to be leaping about like that." Strong hands pushed him onto his back. He wanted to resist but his body failed him. He lay back and felt a cold cloth pressed to his forehead. "That's right. Just relax. You're safe here." The smoky voice was familiar, though he couldn't place it just yet.

"Where am I?" he rasped, scarcely recognizing his own voice. His throat felt like sandpaper and he hurt all over.

"You're at my house. Somebody done messed you up and dumped you in the creek."

Grant blinked to clear his vision and looked at the speaker. The room was dark, with only a sliver of light through the doorway to illuminate it. As his eyes adjusted, he recognized the man.

"Amos?"

"That's me. You're lucky me and my grandson was out catching crawdads when you come tumbling into the water. Whoever done it knew just where the deep place was. You'd have drowned long before you was conscious."

"The Stallards," he croaked.

"I ain't surprised. You didn't really think you could go tooling around town with Jed's girl and them not do something about it?"

"Who, Cassie?"

"Jazy. Everybody knows about her and Jed." Amos cackled. "Lord, his mama don't like it none. A preacher's son going around with the town mattress."

"Wait a minute." Grant sat partway up, supporting himself with his elbows. His head swam, but he ignored it. "Jazy is Jed's girl? But she was the one who..." He shook his head, and pain lanced through his skull. "I don't get it. She practically begged me to take her away for a few days, and was really pissed when I didn't."

"Who knows why that girl does anything? I warned you she was trouble. Now, you need to get yourself some rest. You're bruised from head to toe and I wouldn't be surprised if you got a cracked rib or two."

"I can't." He forced himself up to a sitting position and gasped as a new wave of pain shot through his body. "You know Cassie Brunswick, don't you?"

"Sure do. Good girl, bad life." His assessment was as accurate as it was succinct.

"I think something's happened to her." He drew a ragged breath. "I think her dad, Carl, and the Stallards are all in on it." The pieces began to fall into place as he spoke. "Jazy's a part of it too. They tried to tell me Cassie had gone to stay with her aunt, and I thought it was bullshit until Jazy told me the same story. He pounded his fist on the bed. "That's why she wanted me to take her away. They were using her to keep me from looking for Cassie."

"What exactly do you think they've done to her?"

"Amos, have you ever heard of Kaletherex?"

The old man sprang to his feet faster than Grant would have thought possible, turned, and strode to the door. Before Grant could apologize, the light clicked on, blinding him for a moment. When he opened his eyes again, Amos was once again seated in a chair beside the bed.

"Such things are not to be spoken of in the dark." He sighed. "That's a dangerous question, boy. Wallen's Gap's darkest secret."

Grant waited as the old man's eyes took on a faraway

cast.

"Kaletherex is a religion. Nobody wants to talk about it, of course, except in whispers, because there ain't no telling who's in it and who isn't, but everybody walks soft around here."

"What are they about?"

"Nothing good. I did some researching when I was younger, trying to figure it all out. Best I could tell, they get up to some nasty stuff-- animal sacrifice, sex rituals, evil things."

"What about," Grant swallowed hard, "human sacrifice?" He didn't want to think that was the fate planned for Cassie, but he couldn't forget the pictures he'd seen in his father's book.

"Two times, best I can tell. Both times, a young girl went missing and was found much later, all torn up like some wild animal done it. I don't believe it, though, because both times it happened was some of the darkest times in this town's history." He ran a hand across his leathery brow. "People went plum crazy. Children kept having accidents, as they called them. You couldn't leave your house for fear somebody'd rob you blind while you was gone. Old feuds that died a hundred years before sprung back up. It's like all the evil in people's hearts just bubbled to the surface. It lasted until the next full moon, and that was the worst night of all."

"You talk like you were there."

"I was, for the last one. It was 1962." He lapsed into silence.

"What happened?" Grant urged.

"They went wilding. Leastways, that's what some of us called it. All these men in white robes went through town howling at the moon, setting fires, laying hands on any man or woman who dared stick their nose out the front door. Soon as I saw it starting I got home and we hunkered down here and prayed they wouldn't come our way."

"Didn't you have a gun?"

Amos laughed. "I was a black man in Virginia in 1962. A white man could have killed my whole family right in front of my eyes, but if I took a shot at him, I'd be the one going to prison. Yeah, I had a gun, and I would have used it if I had to, but it wouldn't have made much difference. There was too many of them." He looked down at the floor. "Next morning, it was like everybody woke up from a bad dream. People pulled together and rebuilt what had been destroyed, and nobody talked about what had happened."

"You said there was another time this happened?"

"Yes sir. Happened in 1899. Might have been other times in the past, but I couldn't find no records of it."

Grant considered this.

"Was there anything special about those dates? Anything that ties them together?"

"I only come up with one thing. A conjunction." Seeing Grant's confused expression, he continued. "A planetary alignment. Big ones happened in both of those years, right about the times the girls went missing. Of course, it don't make no sense. Kaletherex is about a bunch of crackers putting on robes and doing wrong. Ain't no need to believe in no supernatural." He waggled his fingers as he said the last word.

"Where are my pants?" Grant asked. "There's something I need to show you." Amos nodded at a pile of clothes on the bedside table. Grant fished around and found the finger.

"What the hell is that, boy? You been grave robbing?"

"My father hid this along with a book that I think is important to Kaletherex. It... moves sometimes."

"Sure it does." Amos nodded, as if indulging a small child.

Grant wanted Amos to believe him. He remembered the first time the finger had moved, he'd been thinking hard about Cassie, wondering where she was and if she was all right. He concentrated on her face. *Where are you? Where are you?*

"Jesus God Almighty!" Amos came to his feet, upending his chair, as the finger twitched and pointed. "What did you do?"

"I didn't do anything. I don't understand much, but I can tell you there's more to Kaletherex than just a bunch of rednecks getting their jollies. They're up to something bad, Amos, and they've got Cassie."

Amos ran his hands through his snow white hair and turned on the spot. "Jesus Lord, I didn't believe it. I was sure it was over and done with."

"What?"

Amos let his hands fall to his side. "There hasn't been a grand conjunction since 1962, but there's going to be another one tomorrow night."

Chapter 16

"Amos, we have to find her!" Grant ignored his body's screaming pain and jumped to his feet.

"Now, calm down, son. Let's just think a minute." Amos laid a hand on his shoulder and gently shoved him back toward the bed.

Grant ignored him. "You said the other times this happened, young girls were found mutilated. If they're aiming to do the same thing again tomorrow night, it stands to reason they're going to use Cassie! Why else would they hide her from us?"

Amos shook his head, his face pained. "You really think old man Brunswick would put his own daughter in the hands of them butchers?"

In fact, Grant thought exactly that, and the sudden conviction made him dizzy. He sank back to the bed, one hand pressed to his ribs. "I've looked in his eyes. He's a cold bastard, sure enough. If these Kaletherex people are as crazy as you say they are, then maybe he would. He's one of them, right?"

Amos nodded. "Yep, I reckon he is. And the Stallards. Hell, most of this goddamn town seems to be in on it sometimes."

"What made you think it was over?"

Amos sank his face into his palms, shook his head. "It was fifty years ago. I thought maybe I'd half imagined the whole thing." He looked up, his eyes haunted. "I've kept an eye on things and knew there was another conjunction coming. But everything 'round here seemed to have settled into some kind of normal. I didn't see any signs like something was happening. Most of the people around back then in '62 are dead and gone. But I guess enough of their kids was old enough then and still around now. The Kaletherex thing has been mighty quiet for a long time. I guess I just hoped it was done with."

"Fifty years ago it was a lot easier to keep stuff covered up," Grant said. "These days, news can spread pretty quickly."

Amos nodded sadly and they sat in silence for a while, both lost in their own grim thoughts. Grant pushed the finger back into its tin and the tin back into his jeans pocket. What could they do? Thoughts of his father drifted through his mind. "Hey, did you know my dad?" he asked.

Amos looked up. "Andrew Shipman? Yeah, I knew him a little bit. He was a nice enough fellow. But he started to hang around with the Brunswicks and Stallards and the others. I had a feeling he got pulled into the Kaletherex cult."

"He did. But I don't think he liked what he found. At least, I think he changed his mind about them." Grant tried to order his thoughts, hard as it was with every inch of his body aching and throbbing. "I found that finger in a secret safe in his smokehouse. He had an old, leatherbound book stashed away in there too. I think the book was really important to them, because Mrs. Stallard came around asking about it, and then her sons busted in and stole it back."

"That right?"

"It had to be them. But they didn't find the finger." Grant pointed to the pocket of his jeans. "I can't really explain why, but I'm pretty sure that thing is important, might even help us somehow. I think my father was collecting information, trying to find out how to stop them and they killed him for it."

Amos nodded sadly. "That is entirely possible."

Grant paused. "They said my dad died of a heart attack."

Amos barked a bitter, humorless laugh. "They can say whatever they like, son. The doctor, the sheriff, the city council. They're all either in that cult or controlled by them. Ain't nothing in this town happens without their say so." At Grant's raised eyebrow, Amos flapped one hand. "Oh, you can live your life here peacefully enough if you stay out of their way. They need goods and services and all that same as everyone else. A whole bunch of people live peacefully enough in Wallen's Gap and never cross paths with the cult of Kaletherex. But people disappear if they cause trouble and there ain't many crimes in this town that get investigated like they oughta. Everything gets explained away nice and easy like."

"How can they get away with that?"

"They's all kinds of things can happen to a body in these hills. Hunting accidents, bad falls, snakebites, wild animals, accidental fires, drunk kids running off of winding mountain roads. Everything just common enough to be believed."

Grant stared disconsolately at the floor between his feet. What was he supposed to do now? He couldn't just walk away and leave, he owed Cassie more than that.

Suzanne's words echoed in his mind, *You never finish anything!* Well, he fully intended to finish this, one way or another. But he was scared and not too proud to admit it. And he had precious little to go on. Dark shadows flitted around the edges of his vision. A tugging pulled at his chest, seemingly from the inside. He imagined a black stain trying to push its way out through his ribs. The sensation was nauseating and disconcerting.

"You okay, son?" Amos said, leaning forward. "You look kinda pale there. You should lie down, you took quite a beating."

Grant shook his head. "It's not that." He took a deep breath. Crazy hillbillies doing evil things in the name of their wacko religious cult was weird, but it still fell within the realm of expected human behavior. What would Amos think about what he was about to tell him? "That finger I found, it has an effect on me that I can't really explain. Like it's trying to guide me."

Amos stood, paced a small circle around the room. When he finally looked at Grant, there was no scorn, amusement, or disbelief in his eyes. Strangely, Grant found himself thinking he would have preferred that to the old man's sober expression.

"My Jesus, I could have done lived this lifetime and another without ever seeing that accursed thing and been happy about it."

"Me too," Grant said. He stood, pulled on his clothes, wincing against aches and stabs of pain. "But it's all we have. Maybe I need to find out more about it."

"Was that thing..." Amos swallowed, shook his head, tried again. "Was that thing pointing the way somewhere?"

"I think it's guiding me to Cassie. Whenever I think

hard enough about her, it... points, like that. Part of me just wants to go now, follow it and save her. But we have no idea what we might be walking into."

"We, boy?" Amos's eyes were wide.

"Please, Amos. I'm alone in all this. I need some help. I don't know anyone else."

"I'm an old man, what can I do?"

"I don't know." Grant slipped his shoes on, rose with difficulty, and stumbled toward the door. "Maybe you can help me learn some stuff. Stuff that can help us?"

"That conjunction happens tomorrow night," Amos said, offering him a helping hand as he guided Grant out into a single room with a small kitchen and dining area to one side and a living area on the other. "Hell, it's nearly tomorrow already. You've probably only got the day time to figure out what you're going to do. Maybe you need to consider that there ain't nothing you *can* do."

"I refuse to accept that! I at least have to try."

"I'm sorry, son. I don't know what else to tell you. There's maybe one person anywhere near here that knows more about this stuff than me, but she's..."

Headlights cut across the front window, setting the tattered curtains aglow. Grant stood, but Amos made a calming motion.

"It's just my son," Amos said. "Back from town. He went to get some more bandages and such from the store while I kept an eye on you."

A rill of fear tickled along Grant's spine. "We're not in town?"

"No, we're on the edge of the woods, a couple of miles from town. After spending all day working in the diner, I like me some peace and quiet." Amos went to the door and pulled it open.

A young man stood there, tall and lanky with light brown skin and amber eyes, a rifle cradled in his arms. "Sorry about this, Pops, but we want Shipman."

"What are you talking about, Elijah? Who is we?" He glanced over his son's shoulder and whoever or whatever he saw there made him gasp, his eyes wide.

"Come on out!" another voice yelled. The unmistakable burr of Jesse Stallard. "We got unfinished business with Shipman. Give him over and we'll leave you alone, Amos."

Through the front door, Grant saw several silhouettes out front, stark against the headlights of a truck.

Elijah gave his father a shove and Amos staggered backward, colliding with a small dining table. He turned to Grant, and pointed at the back door. "Run!" he gasped.

Grant took a step toward the door and froze as Elijah leveled his rifle at him. His son distracted, Amos grabbed a wooden chair and swung it with surprising strength.

The upswing caught Elijah's forearm, knocking the rifle barrel upward as he pulled the trigger. The shot went off with an ear-shattering report, and the ceiling light exploded in a shower of sparks, plunging the small house into darkness.

With a grunt of fear and frustration, Grant turned and groped for the door handle. He cried out as a hand grabbed his upper arm and dragged him to one side. "It's me," Amos hissed.

The headlights of the truck outside arced through

the door, casting long, confusing shadows. People pushed and shoved to get into the house. "Fuckin' shoot 'em both!" someone yelled.

Rather than coming after them, Elijah turned and stumbled toward the door, cradling one arm in the other. "Not my Pops!" he shouted.

Two gunshots rang out and wood chips exploded from the wall by Grant's face. He jumped aside, half-pulled by Amos, and cracked into the door Amos pulled open. They tumbled through with the sounds of scuffling behind them. Three more shots barked out in the darkness accompanied by fiery flashes. Amos yelped, but pushed on, slammed the door behind them. "There!" He pointed across the small yard to a Yamaha trail bike parked up near the tree-line. "Key's in it. You can ride, right?"

Crashing noises came from the house as they ran across the scrub and dirt, ducking into shadows.

"You have to come with me," Grant said. "They'll hurt you if you stay."

"My own goddamn son." Amos's voice dripped pain.

"I know, but it was me he was giving up, not you. He tried to protect you." Grant jumped onto the bike and turned the key. His thumb found the starter and it roared into life.

"I didn't raise him to fall in with fools like that!" Amos said.

The back door burst open and gun barrels swung towards them.

"Get on!" Grant screamed and the old man swung a leg over the pillion seat. As soon as his weight hit the bike, Grant opened it up and fishtailed across the dirt, wincing at the sound of rifle shots. He headed for the trees, Amos hanging on valiantly, one arm tight around Grant's waist.

The bike slipped and skidded, tires spinning for grip on the loose earth. With sheer force of will and more than a little luck, Grant managed to control it and speed into the woods. He was thankful for the half a dozen sessions of mini-motocross he'd insisted on as a kid. He flicked on the headlight and tipped left and right as guns fired and bullets bit chunks out of the tree trunks by their heads. Hoping he could out-run and out-maneuver their shooting, he powered through the forest, up the mountain.

Chapter 17

The gunshots stopped as they barrelled up the steep incline behind Amos's house. There was no way the Stallard's truck could follow them through the dense woods, but Grant had no idea where they were or where to go. "You okay?" he shouted over his shoulder, slowing to a safer pace to navigate the trees.

"Those bastards got my son." Amos said weakly, barely audible over the bike's engine.

"I know, I'm sorry. But if we stop them, you'll get your son back." Grant felt terrible laying his own agenda over the old man's grief, but it was the truth.

"I should kill every last one of those Stallards and Brunswicks," Amos said. "Those families are the heart of all this. Always have been."

"So we need a plan. Where to?"

"Just keep heading up. Soon enough you'll hit a fire trail. When you do, turn left."

Grant followed the simple instructions. Sure enough, a scrubby track soon appeared across their path and he turned onto it, grateful for a reprieve from tree dodging. They rode more sedately as the trail wound slowly up the mountain at a shallower gradient. Amos lay heavy against Grant, his one-armed grip weakening. "You okay?" Grant called back to him.

"Soon enough there's a fork in the trail," Amos said. There was a disturbing slur in his voice. "Take the right fork and head on up till you find a cabin. Ma Withers lives there."

"Ma Withers?"

Amos nodded weakly against Grant's back. "She's a witch. And she's older'n the hills themselves. But if anyone knows more than me about this stuff, it's her. Mind you, she's plum crazy too."

"Will she help us?"

The old man didn't answer.

Grant tried to see back, but couldn't turn and safely control the bike. Gritting his teeth, anger a red heat in his gut, he powered on up the trail. *Hang on, Amos*, he thought. *Please hang on.*

The fork appeared after less than a mile and Grant turned up the mountain. The trail got thinner and rougher and the trees denser. How could anyone live all the way out here? He slowed enough that the bouncing suspension didn't dislodge the old man from behind him and prayed the cabin wasn't far. He was rewarded a few minutes later as the trail opened into a natural clearing and a moss-covered, broken-down building stood bathed in moonlight. It looked like little more than a garden shed, but there was candlelight flickering inside and a figure stood on the small front porch. As Grant pulled the bike up, the headlight illuminated the oldest person he had ever seen. Shrunken with age, bent over, stick-thin, bald and toothless, the woman looked barely human. Her skin was a deep mahogany, striped with more wrinkles than Grant would have imagined possible, hanging off her spindly bones like parchment.

Grant pulled the bike up and killed the engine, silence settling quickly over the woods. "Ma Withers?" he asked.

"Get him in here, he's hurt." The old woman turned back into the hut.

As Grant put the bike onto its stand, Amos slid sideways off the seat. Grant jumped off and caught him. The old man's left arm was soaked in blood, the sleeve of his shirt dark with it. It dripped off his fingertips. Grant picked him up with a grunt and turned for the cabin.

"My own son..." Amos mumbled. His eyelids flickered like he was having a bad dream.

At least he was still alive. Grant carried him inside and was assailed by a harsh, smoky smell that made his eyes water. Ma Withers walked circles around a table in the middle of the room, wafting a bunch of burning leaves in the air. She pointed to the table and carried on circling, muttering words Grant couldn't understand. He laid Amos down on the table and took the old man's shirt off. There was a broad gash across Amos's upper arm, the skin red and angry either side of the welt. It bled heavily.

Ma Withers pushed Grant aside and dropped the remaining smoky leaves into a copper pot under the head of the table. She pulled out a box of bottles and rags and set to work on Amos's wound. Grant retreated to a rocking chair in one corner and sat, watched her work. His body thrummed with the pain of his own injuries, but he ignored them, intent only that Amos would be okay.

Before long the old woman stepped back, looked at her handiwork and nodded. She pulled a kettle from over the open fire in one corner of the shack and poured hot water into a tin mug. "Help me here, son," she said.

Grant stood, lifted Amos's shoulders to a half-sitting position and Ma Withers tipped the mug against his lips. He moaned and liquid ran over his chin. There must have been something already in the mug as the liquid was dark and foul-smelling.

"Drink, son," Ma Withers said, her voice soft and musical.

Amos opened his mouth and sipped. She tipped the mug up and he gulped until it was empty. He sighed as Grant laid him back down and was almost immediately sleeping, his chest rising and falling in a slow, gentle rhythm.

"Thank you for helping us," Grant said. "I'm glad you were up. You seem strangely prepared."

"Ain't nothing strange about it," Ma Withers said, sitting in her rocking chair with a groan. "I got up about an hour ago when I seen you was coming. Had plenty of time to prepare."

"Seen we were coming?"

She tapped the side of head with one gnarled finger. "It ain't something I'm about to explain to you, boy. Just accept it."

"Okay. I appreciate it."

The old woman leaned back in her chair, closed her eyes. "So I been seeing those Kaletherex bastards all week, walking roughshod through my dreams. Now I see that you're the connection. You're in deep trouble, eh?"

Grant looked around for somewhere to sit. He was bone-tired and every part of him hurt. As the excitement of their flight from the Stallards dissipated, his whole body began to tremble. He sat heavily on the edge of the small bed, the only other furniture in the one-room house. "Yes, ma'am, I'm in trouble. I'm sure they have Cassie and I think they mean her harm."

"What's that in your pocket?" Ma Withers asked.

Grant dropped one hand to his hip. "How do you...?"

Ma tutted, shook her head. "Just *accept* it, boy. We ain't got time for teachings and history."

Grant pulled the small tin from his pocket and took out the blackened finger. He held it up and Ma Withers leaned forward to see, squinting so much her eyes seemed to disappear in folds of skin.

"Where'd you get that?"

Grant told her everything. The book, the finger, Cassie, the Stallards. She listened, nodding occasionally, sometimes flapping her hand at him if he went on with too much detail.

Eventually she sighed and smiled. "Well, that finger you found is probably the one piece of good luck you've had, boy. But it'll cost you."

"Cost me?"

"That kind of power never comes without a price. Maybe we *should* make time for some history. Let me tell you a little bit about Josiah Brunswick. You see, he was a powerful warlock and probably the best thing to happen to Wallen's Gap. The original people here, they set up a small town but they were a deviant bunch. They worshiped an evil demon by the name of Kaletherex and the reason they set up a home here in the mountains was in order to commune with their evil god at their leisure. See, when they first came here, this place was in the middle of nowhere, but civilization has a way of catching up to people whether they like it or not.

"Anyway, they set up here and they worked hard at pleasing their demon lord and eventually they managed to raise that black-hearted son of a bitch to what they call corporeality. He actually came from hell to this world and did them favors. Course, you don't play with a demon and keep your mind intact and it drove people mad, but it gave them power too. They got all kinds of boons from their ministry as long as they kept the demon fed. And it only liked to eat the flesh of its most pure followers. Oh, don't frown and wince, boy, you know you're in something deep and evil here. Just accept it and listen.

"The story goes that old Josiah Brunswick heard tell of what was happening up here and his crusading warlock urges drove him to come and sort it out. Now I don't know exactly what he done, but he got in with the townsfolk and lived among them for a while as he learned all about the situation. He even had himself relations with one or two of the ladies and that's kinda his biggest mistake, but we'll get to that. He realized that this little mountain town was only the beginning and if Kaletherex was left to grow and gain power, it would soon devour this place and move on. The stronger it got in the human realm of existence, the more of this world it would want and the more it would get. Old Josiah Brunswick saw Armageddon being born and he fixed to stop it.

"But it was gonna cost him his life. See, he figured out that the only way to defeat this demon Kaletherex was to poison it here in our world and send it permanently back where it came from. So he offered himself up for sacrifice. He played the part of the zealot, the crazy advocate of the demon, so desperate to serve that he wanted to be fed to it. Now the demon will consume any flesh it's offered, so it took old Josiah up gladly, but the brave damned warlock had set spells and charms into himself before the sacrifice and those enchantments exploded inside that demon and carried it straight back to hell and Josiah Brunswick with it, poor bastard.

"But the legend has it that old Josiah left a small part of himself in this place, as a kind of anchor of the flesh, just in case something went wrong and anyone needed some of his power again. So I think that what you have there is old Josiah Brunswick's finger."

Grant sat open-mouthed, his head swimming with the things the old woman had said. It was hard to believe any of it, but given what he had experienced so far, he had little choice. As Ma Withers herself kept saying, just accept it. "But what am I supposed to do with it?" he asked.

"I dunno, kid. That's for you to figure out."

"You said something about relations with ladies?"

Ma cackled a phlegmy laugh. "Yeah, old Josiah liked the ladies. So much so that he left a few Brunswicks behind in their bellies and that's what gave old Kaletherex a window back here. See, he's kinda trapped in hell, but whenever them fools make the proper sacrifice during the grand alignment, he gets himself a moon's cycle to play havoc here again. Those cultists discovered it by killing one of the babies he left behind, but they had to wait a few years for a particular conjunction of planets for the power to be strong enough. Since then they've been protecting the Brunswick line and breeding just for to feed their demon god. But they cut it fine this time, got lazy and complacent. It's been fifty years since the last alignment and the knowledge of their rituals nearly died. But fortunately for them there was one virgin Brunswick girl left."

"Cassie!"

"Yep. They ain't many Brunswicks now, excepting for Cassie's daddy and a few uncles, and they ain't got no children, though I reckon a couple of them might still be able to get a woman with child. Ain't been many Brunswick girls in a long time. Cassie had a little sister what died as an infant. For now, she's all they got. I've seen 'em in my dreams, preparing her at their rituals in the night, getting her ready. She's a pawn in their game, knows nothing about it."

"She thinks she's been sleepwalking," Grant said.

"Mm hmm. And my dreams told me someone was coming from far away to put a bur under their saddle, but that stuff was never clear to me. I guess that's you."

"You happen to dream about whether I succeed or not?"

Ma Withers chuckled. "Don't work like that, son. Mind, I wouldn't tell you if it did."

Grant looked out the window at the dark sky. "So what can I do? It's happening tomorrow tonight."

Ma Withers shrugged. "Like I said, that's for you to figure out. Or you can just stay here and wait for the month of madness in town to pass. It's a force of nature. A force of unnature, perhaps. If you want to try to stop it, I can maybe help you, but I'm an old witch, and you ain't no warlock, son."

Chapter 18

"I can't leave Cassie. I'll take any help you can give me."
Strangely, Grant found he was unafraid. Perhaps it was
the surreality of the whole situation, or maybe it was
because, deep down, he knew he couldn't survive this
and had already accepted his mortality. He should have
died, beaten and dumped in a creek, but had won a
reprieve thanks to Amos. He knew he would never be
able to live with himself if he just walked away now, not
after everything that had happened. So better to die
trying than live in shame. For once, he was going to see
something through, no matter how hard it got.

"I'll do what I can for you, then," Ma Withers said,
"but it might not be near enough. Now, the first thing
you got to do is eat something and get you some rest."
She saw the argument in his eyes and hushed him with a
raised, crooked finger. "You ain't in a fit state to do
nothing for her right now, and neither is Amos. Besides,
they can't do nothing 'til the convergence tomorrow
night. Cassie won't even be there yet. They'll be keeping
her somewhere til then."

Grant nodded reluctantly. She made sense, though
he hated the idea of waiting.

"That'll be just fine then. I need some time to make
ready anyhow." She tottered off and returned minutes
later with a mug of broth, two slices of buttered bread,
and an apple. Grant devoured the meal as if it were his

last, which it might be. Finally, he accepted a steaming cup that smelled of mint, a concoction, Ma Withers said, that would both help him sleep and dull the worst of his pain.

"But if the Stallards come..."

"They ain't comin." She tapped her head. "I would know if they was."

Grant slipped into a fitful slumber, his dreams populated by a macabre mix of gun-toting hillbillies, masked cultists, and demons. When the crow of a rooster woke him, he was surprised to discover that, despite his dark dreams, he felt rested. He'd risen and taken half a dozen steps toward the front porch when he realized the pain from his many injuries was nearly gone, with only a dull ache to remind him of their presence.

Amos and Ma Withers sat on the front porch sipping coffee from cracked mugs. By his relaxed expression, Amos seemed to be feeling the benefits of the old woman's potions, as she called them, as much as Grant was.

"Thought you was gonna sleep all day," Amos wheezed.

Grant couldn't help but grin. Only the faintest hint of the coming dawn glowed amongst the dense trees, lending the world an ashy gray undertone.

"Well, I'm up now, and we need to make a plan. That is, if you're still willing to help me."

"Them sumbitches done seduced my son. I mean to make 'em pay."

Grant nodded. "We've got to figure out where they're taking Cassie, and maybe we can ambush them on the way in. I imagine they'll be on their guard once they get started. Maybe even before."

"I believe I knows exactly where they's going to take her." Ma Withers grinned. "The girls who died was found in the same place, and it ain't too far off from here. You can get there in a day, easy. But first off, we got to get you ready."

She ushered Grant back into the house and sat him on the floor in front of the fireplace. With bit of charcoal, she drew a circle on the floor around where he sat, then scratched out four straight lines.

"Are you drawing a pentagram?" He was unable to keep a bit of nervousness from his voice.

"A pentacle," she corrected. "And I don't want to hear no foolish notions about Satanism and evil. It be a tool like any other. I won't close it off 'til it's time." She moved to the fireplace where a small, cast iron kettle hung. Then, one by one, she took down several old mason jars that lined the mantle, drew a pinch of the contents from each, and dropped it into the kettle, whispering to herself as she worked. Grant caught a few phrases here and there.

"Oxeye and bloodroot to give you strength. Rattlesnake master to make your bite deadly." He heard her name other plants or roots as she sprinkled the leaves and powders. Most were unfamiliar: stonecrop, Adam's needle, lizard tail, Jacob's ladder.

The contents began to smoke, filling the cabin with a cloying scent that made him wrinkle his nose. Ma Withers reached into an apron pocket and dug out one of the tiny New Testaments like the Shriners handed out at parades. She flipped through it until she found what she was looking for, tore out the page, and tossed it into the kettle.

"Can't hurt," she said with a grin. "Now, give me Josiah's finger."

"What?" Grant blinked. He didn't know why, but he was reluctant to part with it.

"Fool boy, I only need a touch of it. Come on now." She snapped her fingers and Grant hesitated only a moment longer before taking out the finger and handing it over to her.

It contorted wildly in her hand, like a worm trying to flee from the fish hook. Using a paring knife, she scraped a few flakes of the withered flesh into the pot, then spat into it before handing the finger back to Grant. Next, she pricked Grant's finger with the tip of the knife. He watched in fascination as his blood welled on the flat of the blade. This went into the pot as well, followed by a splash of water. She gave it three stirs in each direction with a wooden spoon before turning to Grant.

"It be time." She leaned down and drew the final line of the pentacle. As she did so, Grant felt a shiver run down his spine, and the air around him seem to thicken.

Ma Withers dipped her finger into the pot, drawing out a heap of black goo. Muttering words in a language Grant had never heard, she anointed his forehead with the foul smelling paste, then pulled up his shirt and drew a symbol over his heart.

She added water to the kettle and stirred until it roiled and steamed.

"Now, you need a weapon." She pulled an old Bowie knife down from the mantle. The blade was a good ten inches long and rounded at the end, and its razor sharp edge gleamed in the firelight. Its spine was thick and straight, the last two inches curved inward and sharp, making the knife double-edged at its tip.

Slowly, like Achilles' mother dipping him into the river Styx, she coated the blade in the liquid. Holding it up, it seemed to Grant that it glowed faintly, though it was probably just the firelight glistening on the blade. When it was dry, she slid it into a battered leather sheath and set it aside.

"Last thing, just in case the blade don't work." She added cold water to the kettle, tested it with her finger, then upended it over Grant, chanting strange words, their meanings seeming to hang just beyond comprehension.

Grant shivered as the lukewarm water soaked him to the bone. He soon realized he wasn't trembling due to the temperature, but from something else. Whatever spell Ma Withers had cast, he could feel it working. He felt powerful. Was that what made him quake?

And then he remembered why he had undergone this macabre baptism. If he couldn't save Cassie, couldn't stop Kalatherex from rising, Grant himself would be the sacrificial lamb, the poison pill, like Josiah Brunswick. An icy wave of fear rolled through him, and he knew exactly why he trembled.

Chapter 19

Amos looked him up and down when he emerged into the cool light of dawn. "The hell happened to you?"

Grant smiled. "I've been prepared. I'm glad you knew Ma Withers. I feel like we've got a fighting chance."

The old woman followed him onto the front porch. "Things happen for a reason at their intended time, son. You happened for a reason, Cassie did too. And the complacency of the fools in town as well. Question is, whether you can make the best of it or the worst. Ain't no justice to who prevails in things like this, evil wins out as often as good."

Grant frowned, scratched nervously at his hair where the witch's concoction dried. "Thanks for the vote of confidence."

"All I done is get you ready as best I can. I don't even know if any of it is gonna help. I ain't the warlock my grandaddy was."

Grant and Amos both turned sharply to stare at the old woman. "Grandaddy?" they said in unison.

Ma Withers smiled and sat down.

"But that would make you..." Grant started.

"Old as sin and twice as deadly," Ma said with a wicked grin. "That's right. But enough of that. Like I said, I can't guarantee nothing I did is gonna help you, but we can hope it does. If we're all lucky."

"So what now?" Grant asked. "Where now?"

"They's place called Natural Bridge Caverns," Ma said. "It's part of a big old tourist attraction."

"Used to take Elijah there when he was a young 'un." A wistful smile crept across Amos's face, then crumpled in a wave of sadness.

Ma Withers nodded. "Most folk around here do. But there's more to the caves than most folk know about and the dead girls before was always found on the other side of that mountain. They's caves back there that's not on the tourist maps. They's tight, twisting passages a man can barely squeeze through, and dropoffs down into nothing. Too dangerous to let people wander in there. It's fenced off, but I got me a hunch them fools use those caverns for their rituals." She grimaced as she said the last word. "Josiah Brunswick wrote a little bit about it. I can't say I know it for sure, but I'll bet my pinky toe and one of my own fingers that's where they'll be taking Cassie."

"We have nothing else to go on," Grant said. "I suppose we have to try."

Ma Withers went inside to find some paper and a pen and sketched a hasty map of the surrounding country, though Amos insisted he knew the way. It wouldn't be easy to get to the caves she had talked about, as it was several miles hike across some rough country. The only other way in was a drive into town, then back up the valley along a dirt road, but Grant was not prepared to risk a run-in with the Stallards or Brunswicks beforehand. They had already shown the night before that they were happy to shoot him on sight, and he didn't fancy his chances on a narrow road in broad daylight, and he was certain they'd have the road guarded.

After some more sketching and talking, they had a route planned and Ma Withers gave them some more bread and fruit for the journey.

"You know, you 'uns could just sit up here with me and wait til it's all over," she said as they prepared to leave. "This town has an uncanny way of forgetting all about the mayhem once it's done and gone."

Grant shook his head. "Not this time. Fifty years ago, maybe, but this town is more connected to the world now and things will get messy. And besides, I simply cannot let Cassie be killed by a demon!"

"And I mean to save my son before he's in so deep there ain't no saving him," Amos said, his eyes hard.

"I had to try." Ma Withers smiled and put a bony hand on each of their shoulders. "Well, I done my best and I'll sit here and hope it's enough. You're two strong young men, in mind and body." The corner of Amos's mouth twitched upward at being called young. "You just might can finish what old Josiah started. You realize, now, that as long as there's a Brunswick left alive with a drop of Josiah's blood, it ain't over."

They stood in silence for a moment, taking in the implications of Ma's words.

"You mean, without that bloodline, there's no chance of Kaletherex ever coming back?"

"That'd be exactly what I mean. Right now, Cassie is the only virgin girl child left. If she were to, say, lose that virginity..." Ma gave Grant a broad wink.

"Well, I don't know." Grant cursed the hot red flush he felt run up his cheeks.

"Oh, who do you think you foolin', boy? You sweet

on her something fierce. And I reckon she done cottoned to you too." She flapped a hand at any further protestations. "Any how, that's but one line of attack. You gotta make sure her daddy can't never make another daughter. You know what I mean." It wasn't a question. "And when you get out of this, you take that girl as far away from Wallen's Gap as you can, and keep your babies away as well." Ma Withers' face was suddenly serious. "Else Cassie can't be allowed to survive neither."

"They's other Brunswick kin around here," Amos said. "All them white folks got their family trees twisted up together."

"They's some." Ma Withers nodded slowly. "But not near as many as you think. I know who all is left, and I reckon they all gonna be there tonight."

Grant looked at the floor, overwhelmed by the possibilities. "I'm going to save Cassie, and help Amos save Elijah. I just don't know if we would even be able to start killing people left and right. I'm not a murderer."

"It ain't murder to kill the foxes when they in your hen house." Ma shrugged and patted his shoulder. "I just wants to make sure you going in with open eyes. Now good luck to you both. My thoughts is with you, for all the good they're likely to do."

Grant leaned down and kissed the old woman on the cheek. "You've done more than enough already, thank you. You've given me a chance."

"That finger you got gonna cost you, don't forget that. But it could save you too."

Grant nodded, unsure just how the finger might cost him, but he chose not to think too hard on it. How could he possibly plan for what lay ahead of him? He had a weapon, and a place to take it. Beyond that, he would have to react to things as they happened and hope he came out on top. "Thank you," he said again.

Ma Withers nodded, but her face was sad. Her eyes, hooded in their myriad folds of dark skin, were wet and she looked more tired than anyone Grant had ever seen.

"You ready, Amos?" Grant asked.

"Ready as I'll ever be. God and Jesus almighty, I wish I was doing about anything right now but what we're planning."

"Me too, but I guess we don't have any choice."

"All things happen for a reason," Ma Withers said, her voice barely above a whisper.

Grant and Amos turned towards the trees and headed off across the clearing. A knot of doubt and fear in Grant's gut weighed him down, but he did his best to ignore it as they strode into the forest.

Ma returned the two men's waves as they disappeared into the trees, and sat heavily into a small chair on her front porch. She had never been so tired, but it had been a long time since she had felt this much at peace.

"I done all I could for you, Grandaddy," she said in a weak voice. "I think I finally earned me a proper rest."

She looked out at the trees, at the sunlight dappling through the leaves. Birds sang and a soft breeze rustled through, carrying with it the scent of bark and loam. She had never seen beyond this day, even in her clearest dreams. Grant looked to be every bit the hero she had thought he would be, though he was a far sight younger than she had expected. Dreams and portents were never really clear enough, never gave any true detail. But she had played her part and now Grant and Amos would have to play theirs. She had never been able to see what lay beyond this moment and she was happy with that. She didn't want to see any more. She had hope.

Ma Withers closed her eyes and breathed deeply of the mountain air. Slowly the rise and fall of her chest slowed, became shallower and shallower, until it didn't rise again.

Chapter 20

Grant and Amos hiked through rough country in the shade of the dense forest. Ma's map and Amos's innate local sense of the landscape meant they never worried about reaching their destination, but the trek was longer and more arduous than they had expected. Amos kept reminding Grant that he was an old man and Grant reminded him that for an old man who had been shot the day before, he was doing pretty well.

The day began to wane as they pushed on toward the other side of the mountain. Dusk came early among the high mountain peaks and dense trees. Grant endured the increasing sense of dread that sat in his gut like a rock and threw himself into the physical exertion to help ignore it. He felt like a condemned man, each step bringing him closer to his demise, yet there was something satisfying in that. For the first time in his life he had a true purpose, an unquestionable destiny. And while that destiny almost certainly ended with his death, it gave him a sense of relevance that he had never felt before. If this would be the end of his life, it would be a short life indeed, but one with more experience than many people ever saw in their three score years and ten.

It was near sundown when they finally crested a ridge and saw a deep, narrow valley slicing through the mountain below. Grant pulled Amos to a stop and crouched low in the scrub. He pointed.

"People down there. And look, you can see a dark hole between the trees. A cave entrance?"

Amos squinted through the lowering sun. "Sure looks like it. That fellow there is distant kin to the Stallards, and the pretty thing next to him is his wife." He sucked his teeth in disapproval. "I thought they was all right. That woman is a Sunday School teacher, and not at the Stallard's church, neither."

Grant raised an eyebrow. "Really? Seems Ma was right when she said this whole town was in on the thing. How come you've never been drawn into this?"

Amos gestured at his old, wrinkled face. "A black man might have a better life in a town like this than he used to, but he ain't no equal member of society. Too many people got fond memories of segregation, if you catch my drift." He chuckled ruefully. "I reckon this old skin served me well."

"Not so much your son, I guess."

"When Doctor King pictured children of all colors joining hands, this ain't what he had in mind." Amos looked at the forest floor, and shook his head. "I used to pray that my boy wouldn't have a life like mine, could just be seen as a man like anybody else. Didn't ever think I'd curse society for including him. But Elijah is a good boy. He got proper home training. I don't understand why he did this."

"Maybe he was desperate to fit in, to be accepted in his home town. And maybe was proud to have succeeded. Only, this town isn't really the kind of society you want to be accepted into."

Amos nodded, still looking down. "He tried to save me even though he was prepared to give you up. He's brainwashed by these fools, but there's goodness in him yet. I have to believe there is."

"I'm sure you're right. We'll get him out of this." Grant winced internally at the inadvertent lie he had told. What chance did he have of surviving this himself, let alone saving Cassie and Elijah too? But he was not about to give up without trying.

They moved along the ridge to get a better view and a track became clear through the trees below. The path wound down the hillside to the cave mouth, where two burly men, both armed, stood guard at either side. The Stallard cousin and his wife went into the caves after a brief friendly chat with the guards, though Grant and Amos were too far away to hear what they discussed.

Revulsion curdled Grant's stomach as he watched these carefree people acting as if this occasion were no more grave than a family picnic. The fact that they were about to do murder seemed not to occur to them, or if it did, they didn't care.

Grant and Amos moved further down, careful to avoid fallen branches that might give them away with a sharp crack in the still air. When they were only twenty yards or so above the guards they hunkered down again. Amos tapped Grant's shoulder, pointed. Two more people made their way along the track.

"Howdy boys," said one. "It's a fine evening for it, ain't it?"

"You're late," one of the guards said. "Cuttin' it damn close. Better get inside."

"Really? We the last to arrive?"

"Pretty much. Everyone else is inside and we're only waiting on Jed and Jesse, then we start."

Grant's hackles rose at the mention of the Stallard

brother's names. He bit down on anger and waited.

"How long till the conjunction?" one on the track asked.

"Half an hour, maybe? Now get inside."

The men looked at each other, clearly surprised, and hurried in.

Grant turned to Amos, his eyes wide. "I thought we had until tonight," he whispered.

Amos shrugged. "I guess a planetary alignment don't have to wait for night to be in effect."

"We have to hurry!"

Amos pointed at the guards still standing by the cave entrance. "And do what?"

Grant fumed. He felt at once empowered by Ma Withers' ministrations, and simultaneously useless and weak. They had one bowie knife between them against a whole town with guns and a demon on their side. He almost laughed aloud at the absurdity of it all. Ma Withers' words echoed in his memory. *Things happen for a reason at their right time, son. You happened for a reason, Cassie did too.*

Maybe there was something beyond him on his side and this was the right time. More of Ma's words worried at the back of his mind. *Ain't no justice to who prevails in things like this, evil wins out as often as good.* Well, fuck it all. There was just as little justice for these evil bastards as there was for him and maybe one angry young man was all the catalyst needed to make a difference.

"I need to get inside," he whispered. "I've no idea what I can do in there, but I certainly can't do anything from out here."

Amos nodded, looked along the narrow valley trail.

"I'll make you a distraction. Draw those guards away from the cave entrance. When they move, you slip in behind."

"And what about you?"

"I'm a fair woodsman. I'll take my chances."

Grant reached out and shook Amos's hand. "Thank you, Amos, really. You've been more than good to me."

"You just make sure it's worth something, son."

"We will."

Amos nodded once and slipped away between the trees without another word.

Grant sat on the dry ground and breathed deeply, trying to prepare himself for whatever he might find inside the cave. The rock of fear and doubt swelled outward, anxiety-fueled energy surging through his chest and limbs. His eyes sharpened and he felt a sense of purpose and clarity of vision unlike anything he had known before. He pulled old Josiah's finger from its tin and it danced and writhed in his grip, gesturing frantically at the cave mouth. He smiled and put it back into his pocket, not bothering with the tin. The furious squirming of it against his hip was empowering. "Come on, Josiah," he whispered to it. "Let's see if we can't finish this thing."

A voice rang out from away down the trail. "Hey, you two. Help me here! Jesse's hurt!"

Grant squinted into the trees. From his vantage point he saw Amos away down the trail, doing a passable impersonation of Jed Stallard. The two guards exchanged a surprised look. To Grant's chagrin, only one of them left his post. He saw Amos duck into the trees and hightail it up the valley side, the lone guard moving in his direction. Grant would have to finish the other man.

He picked up a stone the size of his two fists, and looked down at the lone remaining guard, who gazed off in the direction his partner had gone. His pistol was holstered, his thumbs tucked into his belt. If Grant were fast, he had a chance. Hefting the rock, he crept down the slope toward the man below. The soft, loamy earth masked the sound of his approach. He was almost directly above the cave mouth when he dislodged a pebble, sending it bouncing down with a clatter that his nerves amplified into a rumble like a landslide.

The guard turned around, more curious than alarmed. His eyes widened when he saw Grant. He fumbled for his pistol, but Grant was already flying through the air. He brought the rock crashing down on the man's head. The fellow crumpled to the ground, his limp body cushioning Grant's fall.

The guy was too big and too heavy for Grant to do a proper job of it, but he managed to drag the unconscious guard into the nearby underbrush where did a half-assed job of covering him in leaves and pine needles. He helped himself to the man's pistol, a snub nosed .38 revolver. The cylinder was full, but the man carried no spare bullets. Obviously hadn't been expecting trouble. Grant imagined there would be a lot more than six people inside, but it was better than nothing.

With a smile and a silent prayer to whatever gods might be listening, Grant slipped into the cool darkness of the cave.

Chapter 21

The orange glow of lanterns set in carved niches cast long shadows as Grant passed from the light of one into the next. He navigated a series of twists and turns, sometimes being forced to scoot along on his belly until, finally, the pass curved slowly to the left and opened up into a huge cavern.

Grant stifled a gasp. Lanterns and candles all around the walls and floor lit the cavern, but still it was so tall that the roof was lost in flickering shadows like squirming ink. Dozens of people stood around the uneven cavern floor, the murmur of low conversation imparting a sense of tense excitement.

Cassie lay on a stone slab in the middle of the floor. She was naked and bound, arms and legs splayed out. Grant ground his teeth, rage boiling inside him at the sight of these sickos looking upon her with undisguised animal longing. Men and women, young and old, it seemed like half the town was here, and dressed in their Sunday best. Cassie looked petrified, tears dripping from the corners of her eyes. Her father stood beside her, his face a mask of zealous pride.

Voices carried along the corridor from behind and Grant hurried behind a rock outcrop at the side of the path, before it descended into the cavern.

"What do you mean hurt?"

"We heard you holler out that Jesse was hurt."

"I did no such thing. You're hearing things."

"Both of us?"

"Well, maybe not. But it don't matter now. Where's Clay?"

"Dunno. He was supposed to stay there, but he must've gone looking for me. Guess it might be that damn Shipman boy."

A bark of harsh laughter. "What is he gonna do?" Grant recognized Jesse Stallard's voice. "Now stand back at your post and if anybody does come by, shoot them in the face. Get on with you, now. It's time."

Moments later, Jed and Jesse Stallard emerged from the passage and strode down into the cavern, passing within less than a yard of where Grant crouched, heart hammering.

"It looks like it's about time," Jesse called out.

Giving her son an approving smile, Mary Ann Stallard broke away from a group of women and moved to her husband's side. They joined hands and moved toward the middle of the cavern, along with Brunswick. Cassie's father smiled at the pastor and nodded, seemingly unbothered by the imminent demise of his only daughter.

Edwin Stallard raised his hands and, slowly, those assembled grew quiet. Unlike the others, he wore a robe like those Grant had seen in his father's book. "Folks, if I might have your attention please. The time of conjunction is upon us and all has been prepared as it needs to be! It's been fifty years since we last had this chance and some of us were just children then, like the next generation here to witness tonight."

He gestured to one side and Grant craned his neck

to see, stunned to spot twenty or more children gathered in the back of the cavern, watching with wide eyes. What kind of thing was this to put in front of kids? Some of them looked as young as two or three. Even the two little girls Cassie minded were there, their faces open and expectant.

"Some of our number were fortunate enough to be involved last time," Edwin went on. He held out one hand to indicate a gathering of old-timers, some being supported by family and friends, too old and infirm to stand unaided. "Brother Jack there stood in my stead last time, blessed with the honor of welcoming Kaletherex into our world. We thank you, Jack."

The old man indicated bowed his head and smiled at the polite smattering of applause.

What the hell was wrong with these people? Grant felt like he'd walked in on a church picnic, not a cult's dark rite.

"And thanks must go to Graham Brunswick," Edwin said, laying a hand on Cassie's father's shoulder. "For it is by his faithfulness that now we have the vessel we require." Brunswick beamed like a praised schoolboy as Edwin Stallard indicated Cassie, tied and terrified beside them. "Ain't she a picture, there," Stallard said.

Cassie stared up at them with terror-filled eyes. "You sick bastards!" she screamed and Grant was proud of the strength in her voice even as his heart swelled fit to crack at her predicament. "Daddy? Why are you doing this to me?" Suddenly, the little girl was so clear in her eyes, even through her terror, that Grant had to look away.

"Now, at long last, the time of the conjunction is once again upon us!" Edwin Stallard cried, reigniting the crowd's zeal. The murmur of voices rose and excitement filled the air again. "All is ready," Stallard went on. "The time has come to draw the blood that shall summon Kaletherex to grace us with his presence and bestow upon us the bounty of his blessings!"

Cheers and applause boomed in the cavern. Grant looked frantically around as the sounds pounded his ears. What could he do? How could he do anything to save Cassie against so many. Several people around the cave had guns in plain sight, rifles and shotguns hanging casually in their arms. He was sure that several more would have small arms concealed on themselves.

"Brothers and sisters, I must now caution you to exercise restraint during this ritual. The life that Brother Brunswick has so generously provided us belongs, not to us, but to Kaletherex. We draw only her blood. He draws forth her life. Only in the desecration of the body may the soul be released to him, and once that gift is given, then shall Kaletherex reward us with his blessing. Remember, do no harm to the vessel, for she is Kaletherex's and his alone. And do not come between them, lest you be consumed."

Now everyone did fall silent. A few children inched closer to their parents. Grant felt no sympathy for any of them. They spared not a thought for Cassie, but feared only for themselves.

Cliff Stallard stepped forward, holding a watch high above his head. "Conjunction!"

"At last!" The reverend drew a large, shining knife from his belt and retrieved the tan leather book so familiar to Grant. He held the book open in one hand, his blade in the other.

Grant almost stood from cover, his mind a whirl of

indecision. He'd have to kill the pastor first, then figure it out from there.

Wait, son. Something, somewhere, seemed to speak to him, a voice distant and ethereal. *It is the demon we must fight, not the people.*

We? Grant thought, and he knew Josiah Brunswick was with him. In some manner, the spirit of the old warlock hovered nearby.

Aye, lad, we. When Kaletherex is near, so am I.

Edwin Stallard stood behind Cassie's head, the knife raised high. Somewhere in the depths of the cavern a deep, a sonorous drum beat began, echoing back and forth around the huge space. Every person gathered fell to their knees and began to chant, a rhythmic, repetitive sequence of ugly words. Cassie screamed, and Stallard spoke strange and broken phrases as he read from the book. He drew his knife slowly along her body, raising a line of blood from her navel up between her breasts.

As Cassie's screams rose, the drum beat louder, the people chanted more fervently and a scouring heat swept through the cavern. The air some five yards from Cassie's feet shimmered and flexed, colors danced across each other like sunlight refracted through a lens and a stench of sulphur filled the air. With a crack like lightning and a shock wave pulse of searing wind, something huge, black and terrible stepped into the world.

Chapter 22

Even crouched on the cave floor, the demon Kaletherex stood taller than any man, and was a mass of corded muscle pressed through tight black skin stretched like a dark membrane across its imposing bulk. Its face was bull-like, with a wide, smoking mouth bristling with huge black fangs. Shining obsidian horns curved up from its head, their razor points almost meeting. Long claws glistened from every fingertip and cut into the cavern floor from every toe. The demon threw its head back and cried out to the heavens, the sound reverberating off the cavern walls and drilling through to Grant's terrified soul. It stretched its arms wide and roared again.

The pounding drum redoubled its beat, the chanting rose in pace in and volume, the voices a cacophony of stuttering rhythm. Mesmerized in the ritual, no one appeared frightened.

A man ran forward and prostrated himself at the demon's feet. His wife, eyes wide, grabbed at him, tried to pull him away. Hunger burned in the onlookers' eyes, their faces gleeful, as the creature lifted the man from the floor. He gibbered, frothing at the mouth in his insane zealotry as Kaletherex slid its claws into his gut, twisted slowly, and drew forth a rope of steaming entrails. His shrieks cut off as Kaletherex bit into his throat. The man's wife screamed as the demon ripped her husband to pieces and swallowed large chunks of the man whole.

Suddenly aware of her, the demon clubbed her with her husband's leg, slamming her to the cave floor. She hit the ground, twitched once and lay still.

Graham Brunswick and Edwin Stallard stepped away from Cassie as she screamed and thrashed against the chains that bound her. Kaletherex turned toward her and stepped forward. The lamplight seemed to dim as the demon rose to its full height.

Grant, fighting against nausea from disgust and fear, forced his muscles to work. His heart pounding, blood pulsing in his temples, his stomach an icy mass of terror, he stood and yelled out, "Leave her alone!"

The chanting faltered and eyes turned to see Grant. He stood on the rock he had hidden behind and raised his arms. From somewhere deep within, his voice rose, empowered by the presence in his mind. "I'm here to face you, Kaletherex!"

"It's Shipman!" Reverend Stallard called. "Shoot him!"

A few weapons swung in Grant's direction, but most were transfixed by Kaletherex and seemed aware of nothing else. Grant felt incredibly vulnerable standing so tall and, rather than face the instant death of dozens of bullet wounds, he leapt from the rock and ran for Kaletherex. He emptied the stolen revolver as he ran, unsure if he hit anything as people dove for cover.

Gasps and shouts resounded around the cavern. The demon crouched and roared again, its voice turning Grant's stomach to water, his legs to tissue. He stared into two fiery red, bottomless eyes and his courage deserted him. He saw hell and eternity in those flaming orbs and knew himself to be irrelevant. The gun dropped from his weak fingers.

A shot rang out and Grant winced, but from the corner of his eye he saw Edwin Stallard stagger back, clutching at his chest.

"You crazy ass people done gone too far!" The voice rang out from the tunnel leading to the cavern. Amos! Where had he gotten a rifle? Amos's face was bloody and bruised, his wounded arm scarlet through the dressings, but he was here and fighting.

Grant found strength in the man's devotion and resourcefulness, and leapt to the side just as Kaletherex closed the gap between them and swiped at him with one huge, taloned hand. The pastor's death seemed to break the spell over the crowd, and confusion and panic swept the room. A press of bodies surged between Grant and the demon as people raced in every direction at once.

"Kill them both!" Graham Brunswick screamed over the tumult.

Amos's son, Elijah, armed with a rifle, stood guard near Cassie. As Graham Brunswick raised a pistol to shoot Amos, Elijah yelled out in alarm. "No!" He swung his weapon up and fired at point blank range into Brunswick's chest. The slug tore through Brunswick in a burst of blood and bone, sent him flying backward.

Amos fired again and again, aiming for anyone who held a weapon, and picking off several, as he ran along one edge of the cavern. People screamed and fought, some trying to get away, others trying to take down Elijah or Amos. A scattering of shots rang out as some of the cultists finally managed to fight back, but the chaos prevented them from getting off good shots. Most went wild, ricocheting off the cavern walls, while others took down fleeing townspeople. It was utter madness and, over it all, the demon Kaletherex roared with something like glee. The creature swept a knot of townspeople aside and came at Grant again.

Grant ducked and rolled, the enchanted bowie knife in his hand. As he came up onto his knees he slashed at the demon, missed, and rolled away again. In his peripheral vision he saw one of the Stallard boys take aim at him and, the next instant, a bullet zipped past his nose, cracking into the rock plinth behind him. Fighting a demon while being shot at? No way.

The last remaining cult members were now firing with impunity, and the repeated gunshots made a deafening counterpoint to Kaletherex's roars as they echoed around the cave. Grant spotted Elijah roll to one side and come up behind the plinth. He aimed his rifle over Cassie's thrashing, screaming form and fired a well-aimed shot across the cavern.

Grant never saw if Elijah hit his target. Too late, Grant realized he had been distracted and Kaletherex struck out. One massive, burning hot black arm collected him across his chest and lifted him high, sent him flying backwards through the air. As he flew, he swept the knife around and felt it bite into the flesh of the demon's arm.

As Grant hit the ground with a bone-jarring impact, Kaletherex screamed. The demon's arm was rent from wrist to elbow and the wound poured thick, viscous black blood and steam roiled up like a volcano.

Dragging air into his protesting lungs, Grant grinned. His every nerve was amped, his eyes alive with power. He saw everything. He had wounded it! Deep down, he hadn't really believed it was possible.

Don't let it get to Cassie, the voice in his head hissed. *If it gets her soul, its power will be unstoppable for a moon's turn!*

People struggled to fight their way out of the cavern, but the throng bottlenecked at the narrow passageway. Gunfire reverberated through the chamber, and Elijah still hid by Cassie, sheltering by the stone altar where she lay bound.

Grant ducked under the sweeping arm of Kaletherex once more and rolled nearer to her. "Cut her free!" he yelled. "Get her out of here, it's the only chance we have!"

He moved again, drawing Kaletherex aside, and dashed forward once more. Red hot talons raked across his back and he ducked and slashed out with the knife. He yelped in pain, but felt the blade slice through the demon's flesh once more. Kaletherex shrieked, its gashed thigh bleeding and steaming.

Grant turned to face the demon and Kaletherex halted, staring hard at the knife that had so painfully wounded it twice. The creature tensed and began to circle, not quite fearfully, but carefully.

"Not so fucking harmless, am I?" He wished he felt as brave as he sounded, but he was beginning to worry. Kaletherex was now wary of him, but clearly the wounds Grant had inflicted were far from grave. He'd imagined that a single drop of Ma Withers' potion would, he didn't know, melt the beast like the witch in *The Wizard of Oz.* His own wounds pained him, draining the energy from him. Could he at least keep Kaletherex at bay long enough for Cassie to get free?

And then he realized what Kaletherex was doing. The beast was circling toward the altar. It wanted Cassie.

Grant moved to intercept the beast, and it roared as it stalked closer.

From the corner of his eye, he saw Elijah sawing at Cassie's bonds with a pocket knife. And behind Elijah, Cliff Stallard appeared, rifle raised.

As Grant was about to call out, Amos emerged from shadow and put his rifle to the back of Cliff's head and fired. Cliff's face vanished in a scarlet explosion. A wave of satisfaction washed through Grant, but it was short lived. More shots rang out and Amos's chest burst in twin sprays of blood.

"Amos!" he cried out, his voice echoed by Elijah, who saw his father fall. Cassie rolled off the altar, her bonds cut, as Kaletherex rushed Grant again.

This time, Grant was too slow. The demon's claws raked across his arm, tearing the knife free, and the force of its charge sent him hurtling backward. He flew through the air and hit the ground hard, the air leaving his lungs in a rush. He pushed himself up on his elbows and watched helplessly as Kaletherex charged in for the kill.

Suddenly, the demon froze, flailing its arms around its face as if swatting flies. Grant was suddenly aware of the continued gunfire, and realized the demon was caught in the crossfire between Elijah and whoever had shot Amos. Unlike the wounds from Grant's knife, the bullets did little more than annoy the demon. It turned and charged what it believed were new attackers.

A familiar voice screamed, "No! I'm on your side!" Moments later, Jesse Stallard's broken body flew from the darkness and landed with a wet smack next to Grant.

Grant gazed dumbly at the shredded corpse, unable to summon the strength to fight. He realized the power of Ma Withers' protections at the sight of how utterly Jesse had been destroyed by one of the demon's blows. But even so, the moments of his life were numbered by the seconds it would take for Kaletherex to find and kill the other shooter. Then it would come for Grant.

Someone poked him. Grant looked around, but no one was there. The invisible hand prodded again. He remembered Josiah's finger tucked in his pocket.

You gotta finish this, boy. This ain't no time for dancing. The voice said. *Kaletherex has its vessel on this earth, and I have mine. Don't forget, I am with you!*

A strange calm rose up through Grant, wrapping him in warm detachment. He reached into his pocket and pulled Josiah Brunswick's finger free, gripping it for strength, and hauled himself to his feet. He didn't turn and run, but searched around for his knife. He found it nearby. His fingers closed around the hilt, and he turned to see Kaletherex impale Sheriff Barton on a stalagmite.

"Grant! Come on!" Cassie, leaning heavily on Elijah, was hobbling toward the passage leading out. "We've got to get out of here."

"You go." Wrapped in the void, he scarcely recognized his own voice. "I'll be there soon." The lie left his lips smoothly, and he felt not a pang of regret as he positioned himself in the path of the demon. He would die here, but Cassie was going to get away. His sacrifice, and Amos's, would not be for nothing.

Kaletherex seemed to move in slow motion as it charged. As the beast loomed over him, massive arms wide, Grant let himself be gathered up in its crushing embrace. The heat of the demon's body burned where it touched his skin. Distantly he heard Cassie scream. His flesh blistered, he smelled his hair burning, and the pain, both agonizing and enlivening, pulsed through him. It was all a faraway thing, and he pushed it aside as he stabbed the demon in the face and neck with the tainted blade, keeping its fanged jaws at bay. His blade bit through infernal flesh and bone again and again as the demon howled.

Grant's strength waned with every blow, but he could feel the demon flagging as well. He yelled as he poured the last of his strength into his attack. He buried the blade halfway to the hilt in Kaletherex's skull. The demon's hellish roar struck him like a blow and he lost his grip on the knife as it thrashed about. Grant bounced against the cavern wall, scarcely keeping his feet.

But it wasn't a killing blow. Kaletherex, the bowie knife jutting from its forehead like a twisted unicorn, was still very much alive, and very angry with its tormentor. As the demon stalked forward, the voice came again.

That's not the way, boy. I told you, I am with you.

"What do you mean?" he cried, wondering if Brunswick could hear him. "Tell me what to do! The only thing about you that's with me is this damn finger!" The finger writhed in his grip, as if struggling to reach the demon. "The hell with you, Brunswick," he muttered.

Kaletherex was almost upon him, jaws open wide, ready to devour him. "And the hell with you!" He looked down into the gaping, tooth-filled maw of the demon and laughed maniacally. "Remember Josiah Brunswick? Here's what's left of him, and I hope you choke on it!" He laughed again and thrust the writhing finger deep into Kaletherex's throat.

That's the way, boy! The voice was exuberant, yet

already distant, fading.

Kaletherex roared around Grant's hand in its throat and slammed its mouth shut. Through the pain and stench of burning, Grant vaguely registered his arm as it was severed below the elbow and disappeared into the huge, black beast.

The demon screamed and staggered back. Grant stared wide-eyed at the stump of his left arm, not bleeding, already cauterized by the hell-creature's furnace bite. Kaletherex roared, clutching and clawing at its throat and stomach. Some people still ran and screamed, though there seemed to be hardly anyone left in the cavern but the dead and the gibbering mad.

Pain lanced through every atom of his body, but Grant ignored it. He stumbled to his feet as Kaletherex fell to its knees. The demon swung blows left and right like a drunk swinging desperate punches as the strength left it and its hold on the mortal realm wavered. Its presence shifted and morphed, became gossamer and unreal. Grant grabbed the Bowie knife, yanked it free of the beast's skull, and stabbed and slashed, again and again, until it felt as though he was swiping through nothing but air. With a soul-rending roar of agony and despair, Kaletherex folded in on itself and fell away from the world.

Blackness swimming in from every part of his vision, Grant managed a weak, strangled laugh and let the darkness take him as he fell face-first to the floor.

Chapter 23

Grant vaguely registered sensations of movement, a change in temperature. He heard sounds of the forest and heard distant shouts. Pressure on his body as he was shaken roughly and realized he was being carried over someone's shoulder as they ran. He heard a voice calling his name and some distant part of him celebrated as it was almost certainly Cassie's words he heard. Blackness took him again.

He woke lying on something soft. He registered movement and something brushed the hair from his brow. He opened his eyes and Cassie's face split in a grin of sheer joy.

"You're alive!" she said. She was wrapped in a big, dirty coat.

"Am I?" He saw movement behind her and realized he was looking out the back window of a car. He lay across the back seat, his head in her lap. He turned his head and saw the dark shape of the driver and recognized Elijah's short cropped hair. Tears streaked the young man's cheek as he drove. The passenger seat was empty.

Cassie eyes were sad again. "Your arm..." she said quietly.

Grant tried to grin at her. "Got another," he slurred.

He closed his eyes and let the oblivion of darkness take him again.

The next time he woke, he found himself lying in a hospital bed. Cassie and Elijah sat beside him. Elijah stared into nowhere and Cassie smiled as he found her eyes.

"You're going to be okay," she told him. "But you're badly hurt, so you have to stay still."

He nodded, winced at the movement and stopped. "Yeah. Don't think I'm going anywhere any time soon."

"I can't believe you came for me," Cassie said, looking away, unable to hold his gaze. "You came for me and you fought that thing." She looked back, tears in her eyes. "You beat that thing!"

"I had a lot of help." Grant looked at Elijah. "I'm so sorry about Amos."

Elijah nodded. "I did that to him."

Grant had no idea what to say to that. It was true. But it was also because of Elijah that Amos had come to help and the old man's bravery and fighting spirit made all the difference. "Your dad was amazing. There's no way I could have done what I did without him. He saved all of us, even you."

Elijah nodded again, said nothing. Fresh tears rolled slowly down his cheeks.

"Where are we?" Grant asked Cassie.

"Kingsville. We just drove away from Wallen's Gap, away from all of that and straight here to the hospital. I don't ever plan to go back, either."

Grant's eyes fell on a newspaper lying on Elijah's lap. The headline read *Cavern Collapse!* He recognized a picture of Natural Bridge. "What's that?"

"The cover story. You been out cold for nearly two days." Elijah tossed the paper onto the bed.

A cave-in at Natural Bridge Caverns claimed the lives of dozens of Wallen's Gap residents in the worst tragedy to hit the community in decades. Members of the Wallen's Gap Community Church were enjoying a picnic in one of the larger chambers when the roof suddenly gave way. A representative of the Virginia Department of Conservation and Recreation said that the chamber in question was in a remote area of the park and not a place frequented by tourists. Local authorities…

He stopped reading. They had certainly moved fast. The Kaletherex cult was going to get away with it. To hell with them. If the survivors were willing to be a part of the cover-up, they deserved what they got. He looked at Cassie and grinned.

"What do you say, when I get out of here, we head west until we hit the Pacific? I've had my fill of mountains. Let's see what it's like by the sea."

Cassie smiled, but her eyes reflected the deep injury she had endured, to body and soul. It would be a long time before either of them were even vaguely better. But she seemed to genuinely mean it when she said, "I'd really like that."

"What about you, Elijah?" Grant asked. "You want to come and see the ocean?"

Elijah shook his head. "I got a sister moved to New York to go to college. Reckon I might go and see her, tell her what happened. Then maybe stay there a while if she'll have me."

Grant nodded. He keenly felt the burned patches of

skin, the torn muscles and cracked bones throughout his body. He lifted his left arm, what remained of it, and stared at the dressing that rounded off just below his elbow. So much for his dreams of being a professional musician. Then again, the drummer from Def Leppard only had one arm. A shame Grant was a guitarist. Perhaps Suzanne had left him for all the wrong reasons, but it led him to Cassie. He thought she would support him whatever his dreams. And he would support her.

He remembered Ma Withers' words. *That finger you got gonna cost you, don't forget that.* He hadn't known what she meant, but Grant knew well enough now.

"Your arm," Cassie said, eyes wet as she looked at his injury.

Grant smiled. "I'm just glad to be alive." And he meant it. "I honestly thought I was going to die back there in that cave. I was kind of at peace with that. So seeing as I've managed to get away with nothing but some injuries that'll heal and only ended up losing my hand, I guess I can live with that."

"That's quite an amazing attitude to have."

"Oh, it's going to take some getting used to, I don't doubt that. And I'll be angry about it for a fair while. Just as well I'm right-handed. But any problems I run into, I guess I'm going to need your help."

Cassie leaned forward and kissed him softly. Her lips were warm against his. "I can do that," she said.

Chapter 24

In Wallen's Gap the people moved through the streets like ghosts. A sense of something terrible hung in the air, something lost and broken. For any survivors of the cave that night, little was ever said about what had happened. It took several days to quietly bury the bodies of all the dead. The new sheriff, a swiftly promoted local deputy, spent many late nights organizing the paperwork to hide the events up in the hills beyond town.

In a house up beside the church, Mary Ann Stallard sat stony-eyed across the table from a young girl with red hair and freckles across her nose. "I lost a husband and three sons that night," Mary Ann was saying, "so I ain't about to let you outta my sight."

"You never have," the young girl said, her face sullen.

"Don't give me none of your sass. Your daddy's the one who give you to us for safe-keeping when you was just a babe. We've fed and clothed you and cared for you like you was our own."

"I don't remember any of your own being forced to live in the basement their whole lives."

"That's enough." Mary Ann's voice cracked like a whip. "You know how precious you are." Her face and voice grew dark. "And if the good reverend had controlled his natural urges, we wouldn't have had to use your sister, and maybe my men would still be alive."

"And my daddy," the girl added, though there was no feeling in her words.

"You just look after yourself, and that one there." Mary Ann nodded at the girl's stomach. "Now you make us a fresh pot, ya hear."

The young redhead nodded and rose from the table, one hand resting on her rotund belly.

"Oh, and one other thing," Mary Ann said.

"Yes, ma'am?"

"If that ain't a girl child the good reverend put in there, Sally Brunswick, we're gonna find you a baby daddy to keep on working at you until it is. I don't know if our lord is gone for good or not, but there will be another conjunction and I aim to live to see it."

END

About the Authors

Alan Baxter is a Ditmar Award-nominated British-Australian author living on the south coast of NSW, Australia. He writes dark fantasy, sci-fi and horror, rides a motorcycle and loves his dog. He also teaches Kung Fu. He is the author of the contemporary dark fantasy thriller novels, RealmShift and MageSign, and over 40 short stories which have appeared in a variety of journals and anthologies in Australia, the US, the UK and France, including the Year's Best Australian Fantasy & Horror. Alan is also a freelance writer, penning reviews, feature articles and opinion. He's a contributing editor and co-founder at Thirteen O'Clock, Australian Dark Fiction News & Reviews, and co-hosts Thrillercast, a thriller and genre fiction podcast. Read extracts from his fiction at his website www.alanbaxteronline.com or find him on Twitter @AlanBaxter, and feel free to tell him what you think. About anything.

David Wood is the author of the Dane Maddock Adventures series and several stand-alone works, as well as The Absent Gods fantasy series under his David Debord pen name. He loves history, archaeology, mythology, and cryptozoology, and tries to work all of these varied influences into the Dane Maddock books, in particular. He is a proud member of International Thriller Writers and co-hosts the ThrillerCast podcast. He loves to discuss books and publishing, so feel free to connect with him at **www.davidwoodweb.com** or on Twitter or Facebook.

CPSIA information can be obtained at www.ICGtesting.com
Printed in the USA
LVOW061613160513

334165LV00010B/1192/P